FACE TO FACE

A Collection of Stories

by

Celebrated Soviet and American Writers

Face to Face

A COLLECTION OF STORIES BY
CELEBRATED SOVIET AND AMERICAN WRITERS

ROBERT CORMIER · AKRAM AILISLI · JEAN FRITZ
ANATOLY ALEKSIN · VIRGINIA HAMILTON · GUNARS CIRULIS
WALTER DEAN MYERS · VICTOR DRAGUNSKY · SCOTT O'DELL
YURI KAZAKOV · KATHERINE PATERSON · VILIS LACIS
CYNTHIA RYLANT · RADII POGODIN · CYNTHIA VOIGT
YURI YAKOVLEV · JANE YOLEN · VYTAUTE ZILINSKAITE

Designed by Barry Moser

Edited by Thomas Pettepiece and Anatoly Aleksin

PHILOMEL BOOKS
New York

Published by Philomel Books,
A division of the Putnam and Grosset Book Group
200 Madison Avenue, New York, NY 10016.
Published simultaneously in Canada.
 Book design by Barry Moser.
Printed in the United States of America.

Library of Congress Cataloging-in-Publication Data

Face to face: a collection of stories by celebrated Soviet and American writers, Robert Cormier . . . [et al]/design and calligraphy by Barry Moser: edited by Thomas Pettepiece and Anatoly Aleksin.

p. cm.

Includes index.

Summary: Presents short stories and excerpts from novels by American and Soviet writers.

ISBN 0-399-21951-X

1. Children's stories, American. 2. Young adult fiction, American—20th century. 3. Short stories, Russian—Translations into English. 4. Short stories, English—Translations from Russian. [1. Short stories.] I. Moser, Barry, ill. II. Pettepiece, Thomas. III. Aleksin, Anatolii Georgievich.

PZ5.F16 1990

813'.54'0809283—dc19

[Fic] 89-3874 CIP AC

First Impression

For a brighter peace in every child's heart.

We commend and salute the American and Soviet writers, all of whom are not only masters of words, but active advocates for children, who have graciously donated their stories for this volume. All net proceeds are being donated by the authors, agents, editors and publisher to the U.S. Committee for UNICEF for the work of UNICEF in promoting the health, education, well-being and rights of children around the world.

In addition, we gratefully acknowledge the loving support, professional advice and vision of the following people who have made this volume possible: Tatyana Setunskaya, Committee of Children and Youth Literature of the Union of Soviet Writers; John Archambault, American co-author with Bill Martin of the award-winning *Knots On A Counting Rope;* Patricia Lee Gauch, Editor-in-Chief of Philomel Books, New York; Tracy Gates, Philomel Books, New York; Margaret Frith, President, Putnam & Grosset Book Group, New York; Frieda Lurie, intepreter and expert on American literature with the Union of Soviet Writers; Marat Shishigin, Department Chief of Republic and Regional Publishing Houses and Nickolai Furmanov, Deputy Chief, International Relations Department of the State Committee of Publishing, Printing and Booktrade, USSR; Vladimir Uvarov, Editor-in-Chief, Tamara Shatunova, Director, and the staff of the Detskaya Literature Publishers, Moscow; The Center for Soviet-American Dialogue organizers of the first Soviet-American Citizen Summit.

The Editors

CONTENTS

FOREWORD

BY HUGH DOWNS, CHAIRMAN OF THE
BOARD OF THE U.S. COMMITTEE FOR UNICEF

COMMUNICATION BETWEEN CULTURES and nationalities always has the effect of deepening understanding and promoting mutual security.

The stories in *Face to Face* are not only delightful merely to read, but they reflect the importance of broadening children's awareness of the world.

Some of them (particularly "The Tubeteika Affair") deal directly with this kind of communication. Fortunately, this approach need not be limited to children and, as the world enters a deeper phase of interdependence, anything that enhances understanding among those who share the same concerns for love, peace, and friendship is a most welcome addition to literature.

PREFACE

THE BOOK YOU are holding is making history: It is the first collection of Soviet and American stories for children and youth in one volume published simultaneously in both countries. It represents some of the best contemporary prose stories with humanitarian themes in Soviet and American children's literature.

In an era of glasnost (openness) and increased cooperation between citizens of our two great nations on many levels, we hope it will be the first of many such joint ventures.

The history books and press of both countries have usually emphasized the differences between the Soviet Union and the United States: democracy vs. communism, the arms race, and regional conflicts around the world.

In truth, our peoples and countries are very much alike. Our countries are vast territories, spanning oceans and seas, with a rich landscape of majestic mountains, plains of wheatfields and seashores, rich in natural resources and wildlife. Our peoples speak many languages with great ethnic diversity. They love the arts and sciences. They are creative, talented, loving, caring, family-oriented people who love the vibrancy and diversity of life. They want peace, and many are rejecting the past perceptions of one another as the enemy, the mistrust and ignorance that have only served to separate and alienate us.

Some years ago Yuri Andropov, the General Secretary of the Central Committee of the Communist Party of the Soviet Union and Chairman of the Presidium of the Supreme Soviet, replied to the letter of Samantha Smith, a ten-year-old American schoolgirl from Maine who asked him what his country was going to do to prevent war. In part he said, "We want peace. We have a lot to do: grow grain, build, invent, write books and make space flights. We want peace for ourselves and for all people of the planet, for our own kids and for you, Samantha."

Now it is time to take a closer look into the hearts of one another, as we share our dreams, nurse our babies, pray for our youth, and tend our aged. Together we have a far greater mission: to rebuild our environment and create a just and friendly world for children everywhere.

The words of the outstanding Soviet writer Maxim Gorky are symbolic: "Tell me your attitude towards children, and I'll tell you who you are." Love for young generations is a noble and high feeling. Caring for young people is our sacred obligation. Practically all great masters of words have taken care of the growing generation by building up the moral climate necessary for the hearts and minds of children.

In Russian and American literature there is a common and beautiful tradition. The classics of both countries resound with joy: The wise fairy tales of Pushkin, children's stories of Leo Tolstoy, the humor and wit of Mark Twain, the courage and stories for justice of Jack London. This tradition is carried on with dignity by contemporary writers of both countries.

Every child needs pure love. They also need the respect of adults and true attention to help their dreams and aspirations come true. The best writers for children know this. Care for the well-being of children is the shortest way to mutual understanding and trust between individuals and nations. The way to peace is enhanced by lasting friendships between young people of both our countries and is inspired by the ideals of goodness portrayed in the best books by Soviet and American writers.

The stories we have collected are not political, they are human. Read them, ponder them, savor them, share them. Let the characters come alive in your mind and heart. For these are really not the best stories of two worlds at all. They are the musings of the hearts of one world, calling us to sing with one voice.

The same word is used in Russian for world and peace—"mir." May this volume serve the brotherhood established between our children for peace all over the earth.

ANATOLY ALEKSIN, Soviet Editor
President of the Association
"Peace to the Children of the World"

THOMAS PETTEPIECE, American Editor
President of PeacExpo

BROTHER LEON

Robert Cormier

BROTHER LEON was getting ready to put on his show. Jerry knew the symptoms–all the guys knew them. Most of them were freshmen and had been in Leon's class only a month or so, but the teacher's pattern had already emerged. First, Leon gave them a reading assignment. Then he'd pace up and down, up and down, restless, sighing, wandering through the aisles, the blackboard pointer poised in his hand, the pointer he used either like a conductor's baton or a musketeer's sword. He'd use the tip to push around a book on a desk or to flick a kid's necktie, scratching gently down some guy's back, poking the pointer as if he were a rubbish collector picking his way through the debris of the classroom. One day, the pointer had rested on Jerry's head for a moment, and then passed on. Unaccountably, Jerry had shivered, as if he had just escaped some terrible fate.

Now, aware of Leon prowling ceaselessly around the classroom, Jerry kept his eyes on paper although he didn't feel like reading. Two more periods. He looked forward to football practice. After days of calisthenics, the coach had said that probably he'd let them use the ball this afternoon.

"Enough of this crap."

That was Brother Leon–always trying to shock. Using words like crap and bull and slipping in a few damns and hells once in a while. Actually, he did shock. Maybe because the words were so startling as they issued from this pale and inoffensive looking little man.

Later on, you found out that he wasn't inoffensive, of course. Now, everyone looked up at Leon as that word crap echoed in the room. Ten minutes left—time enough for Leon to perform, to play one of his games. The class looked at him in a kind of horrible fascination.

The brother's glance went slowly around the room, like the ray of a lighthouse sweeping a familiar coast, searching for hidden defects. Jerry felt a sense of dread and anticipation, both at the same time.

"Bailey," Leon said.

"Yes, Brother Leon." Leon *would* pick Bailey: one of the weak kids, high honor student, but shy, introverted, always reading, his eyes red-rimmed behind the glasses.

"Up here," Leon said, finger beckoning.

Bailey went quietly to the front of the room. Jerry could see a vein throbbing in the boy's temple.

"As you know, gentlemen," Brother Leon began, addressing the class directly and ignoring Bailey completely although the boy was standing beside him, "as you know, a certain discipline must be maintained in a school. A line must be drawn between teachers and students. We teachers would love to be one of the boys, of course. But that line of separation must remain. An invisible line, perhaps, but still there." His moist eyes gleamed. "After all, you can't see the wind but it's there. You see its handiwork, bending the trees, stirring the leaves . . ."

As he spoke, he gestured, his arm becoming the wind, the pointer in his hand following the direction of the wind and suddenly, without warning, striking Bailey on the cheek. The boy leaped backward in pain and surprise.

"Bailey, I'm sorry," Leon said, but his voice lacked apology. Had it been an accident? Or another of Leon's little cruelties?

Now all eyes were on the stricken Bailey. Brother Leon studied him, looking at him as if he were a specimen under a microscope, as if the specimen contained the germ of some deadly disease. You had to hand it to Leon–he was a superb actor. He loved to read short stories aloud, taking all the parts, providing all the sound effects. Nobody yawned or fell asleep in Leon's class. You had to be alert every minute, just as everyone was alert now, looking at Bailey, wondering what Leon's next move would be. Under Leon's steady gaze, Bailey had stopped stroking his cheek, even though a pink welt had appeared, like an evil stain spreading on his flesh. Somehow, the tables were turned. Now it seemed as if Bailey had been at fault all along, that Bailey had committed an error, had stood in the wrong place at the wrong time and had caused his own misfortune. Jerry squirmed in his chair. Leon gave him the creeps, the way he could change the atmosphere in a room without even speaking a word.

"Bailey," Leon said. But not looking at Bailey, looking at the class as if they were all in on a joke that Bailey knew nothing about. As if the class and Leon were banded together in a secret conspiracy.

"Yes, Brother Leon?" Bailey asked, his eyes magnified behind the glasses.

A pause.

"Bailey," Brother Leon said. "Why do you find it necessary to cheat?"

They say the hydrogen bomb makes no noise: there's only a blinding white flash that strikes cities dead. The noise comes after the flash, after the silence. That's the kind of silence that blazed in the classroom now.

Bailey stood speechless, his mouth an open wound.

"Is silence an admission of guilt, Bailey?" Brother Leon asked, turning to the boy at last.

Bailey shook his head frantically. Jerry felt his own head shaking, joining Bailey in silent denial.

"Ah, Bailey," Leon sighed, his voice fluttering with sadness.

"What are we going to do about you?" Turning toward the class again, buddies with them—him and the class against the cheat.

"I don't cheat, Brother Leon," Bailey said, his voice a kind of squeak.

"But look at the evidence, Bailey. Your marks—all *A*'s, no less. Every test, every paper, every homework assignment. Only a genius is capable of that sort of performance. Do you claim to be a genius, Bailey?" Toying with him. "I'll admit you look like one—those glasses, that pointed chin, that wild hair . . ."

Leon leaned toward the class, tossing his own chin, awaiting the approval of laughter, everything in his manner suggesting the response of laughter from the class. And it came. They laughed. Hey, what's going on here, Jerry wondered even as he laughed with them. Because Bailey did somehow look like a genius or at least a caricature of the mad scientists in old movies.

"Bailey," Brother Leon said, turning his full attention to the boy again as the laughter subsided.

"Yes," Bailey replied miserably.

"You haven't answered my question." He walked deliberately to the window and was suddenly absorbed in the street outside, the September leaves turning brown and crisp.

Bailey stood alone at the front of the class, as if he was facing a firing squad. Jerry felt his cheeks getting warm, throbbing with the warmth.

"Well, Bailey?" From Leon at the window, still intent on the world outside.

"I don't cheat, Brother Leon," Bailey said, a surge of strength in his voice, like he was taking a last stand.

"Then how do you account for all those *A*'s?"

"I don't know."

Brother Leon whirled around. "Are you perfect, Bailey? All those *A*'s—that implies perfection. Is that the answer, Bailey?"

For the first time, Bailey looked at the class itself, in mute appeal, like something wounded, lost, abandoned.

"Only God is perfect, Bailey."

Jerry's neck began to hurt. And his lungs burned. He realized he'd been holding his breath. He gulped air, carefully, not wanting to move a muscle. He wished he was invisible. He wished he wasn't here in the classroom. He wanted to be out on the football field, fading back, looking for a receiver.

"Do you compare yourself with God, Bailey?"

Cut it out, Brother, cut it out, Jerry cried silently.

"If God is perfect and you are perfect, Bailey, does that suggest something to you?"

Bailey didn't answer, eyes wide in disbelief. The class was utterly silent. Jerry could hear the hum of the electric clock. He'd never realized before that electric clocks hummed.

"The other alternative, Bailey, is that you are not perfect. And, of course, you're not." Leon's voice softened. "I know you wouldn't consider anything so sacrilegious."

"That's right, Brother Leon," Bailey said, relieved.

"Which leaves us with only one conclusion," Leon said, his voice bright and triumphant, as if he had made an important discovery. "You cheat!"

In that moment, Jerry hated Brother Leon. He could taste the hate in his stomach–it was acid, foul, burning.

"You're a cheat, Bailey. And a liar." The words like whips.

You rat, Jerry thought. You bastard.

A voice boomed from the rear of the classroom. "Aw, let the kid alone."

Leon whipped around. "Who said that?" His moist eyes glistened.

The bell rang, ending the period. Feet scuffled as the boys pushed back their chairs, preparing to leave, to get out of that terrible place.

"Wait a minute," Brother Leon said. Softly—but heard by everyone. "Nobody moves."

The students settled in their chairs again.

Brother Leon regarded them pityingly, shaking his head, a sad and dismal smile on his lips. "You poor fools," he said. "You idiots. Do you know who's the best one here? The bravest of all?" He placed his hand on Bailey's shoulder. "Gregory Bailey, that's who. He denied cheating. He stood up to my accusations. He stood his ground! But you, gentlemen, you sat there and enjoyed yourselves. And those of you who didn't enjoy yourselves allowed it to happen, allowed me to proceed. You turned this classroom into Nazi Germany for a few moments. Yes, yes, someone finally protested. "Aw, let the kid alone." Mimicking the deep voice perfectly. "A feeble protest, too little and too late." There was scuffling in the corridors, students waiting to enter. Leon ignored the noise. He turned to Bailey, touched the top of his head with the pointer as if he were bestowing knighthood. "You did well, Bailey. I'm proud of you. You passed the biggest test of all—you were true to yourself." Bailey's chin was wobbling all over the place. "Of course you don't cheat, Bailey," his voice tender and paternal. He gestured toward the class—he was a great one for gestures. "Your classmates out there. They're the cheaters. They cheated you today. They're the ones who doubted you—I never did."

Leon went to his desk. "Dismissed," he said, his voice filled with contempt for all of them.

ROBERT CORMIER

Robert Cormier was born in 1925. All of his thought-provoking novels for teenagers have been named Best Books of the Year by the American Library Association, and his award-winning books The Chocolate War *and* I Am the Cheese *have been made into movies. Robert Cormier has published three novels for adults, and was a prizewinning newspaper writer and editor. He is a gentle, thoughtful, family-oriented man, and he and his wife have raised three daughters and a son and live in the town he was born in, Leominster, Massachusetts,* USA.

WILD ROSEMARY

Yuri Yakovlev

HE OPENLY YAWNED in class. Then he would shake his head vigorously and fighting off sleepiness stare at the blackboard. But in a few minutes he would yawn again.

"Why do you yawn?" Zhenya would ask, annoyed.

She was convinced that he yawned because he was bored. It was useless to question him–he never had much to say. Actually he yawned because he was always sleepy.

Once he brought a bunch of twigs into class, and put them on the window-sill in a jar of water. Everybody made fun of the bunch and somebody even tried to use it as a broom to sweep the floor with.

He recovered the twigs and put them back into the jar. He changed the water every day.

Zhenya was secretly amused.

But one day the "broom" broke into blossom. Little lilac-colored flowers that looked like violets covered the twigs, and light-green leaves like little teaspoons appeared from the swelling buds while the last thawing snow was still sparkling outside. Children crowded at the window to have a look at the flowers and catch their delicate sweet scent. They breathed it in noisily, and wondered what kind of plant it was, and why it was in blossom.

"Wild rosemary," he growled out and went off.

A tight-lipped person evokes suspicion; you never know what's on his mind, whether he means well or ill. So people are wary, to be on the safe side. Teachers do not like children who are reticent and keep mum all the time even though they sit quietly in class. At the blackboard each word has to be squeezed out of them.

When the wild rosemary put forth flowers, the children forgot about the boy's reticence and wondered if he was a magician. Zhenya looked at him with unconcealed interest.

Zhenya was what the children called Evgenia Ivanovna behind her back. They used the familiar diminutive because she was small and slim, had a slight squint, and wore a turtleneck jumper and high-heeled shoes. Nobody would have taken her for a schoolmistress outside school. Look how she tied up her hair in a ponytail, how she ran across the street, her heels tapping on the pavement!

Zhenya noticed that when the bell rang at the end of the last lesson every day, Kosta sprang up from his seat and hurried away at breakneck speed. He clattered down the staircase, grabbed his coat, fumbled with the sleeves without halting, and disappeared through the door. Where was he off to?

He was seen in the street with a light brown dog. Its long silky hair waved like tongues of flame. But later in the day he was seen with another dog. Under its brittle tiger-colored skin, moved the muscles of a prizefighter. And later still he could be observed walking a black piece of burnt-out wood on crooked, short legs. It was not completely black, over its eyes and on its breast some brownish scorch-marks glowed.

And what the kids didn't say about Kosta!

"He owns three dogs!"

As a matter of fact he didn't own any.

Where those dogs came from and what Kosta had to do with them was a secret even to Kosta's parents. There were no dogs at home and there were no immediate plans to get any. When Kosta's parents came back from work they found him at his desk scribbling something in his notebook or learning verb conjugations. He used to sit there till late at night. So what could all those setters, boxers and dachshunds have to do with him?

The thing was that Kosta got home fifteen minutes before the arrival of his parents from work, so that he hardly had time to clean the dogs' hair off his pants.

Incidentally, apart from those three dogs there was a fourth one–an enormous, big-headed beast, the kind of dog that rescues people caught in snow slides in the mountains. Its bony shoulder blades stuck out through its long tangled hair, its big, lion-like paws, with which it could easily knock down any dog, stepped hesitantly and heavily.

No one ever saw Kosta with that dog.

The bell after the last lesson was like a signal flare for Kosta, launching him into his mysterious life about which no one had a clue. However vigilantly Evgenia Ivanovna watched him, the moment she took her eyes off him the boy slipped away, vanished into thin air.

One day Zhenya could stand the mystery no longer. She rushed after Kosta. She ran out of the classroom, her heels tapping on the staircase, and caught sight of him tearing towards the exit. She slipped through the front door and followed him into the street. Hiding behind pedestrians, she ran trying not to tap too loudly with her high heels, her ponytail flying in the wind.

She played at being a sleuth at that moment.

Kosta ran home–he lived in a dilapidated green house–disappeared through the front door, and five minutes later reappeared in the street. That had been long enough for him to drop his bag, gulp down his cold lunch, and stuff his pockets full of bread and the remains of his lunch.

Zhenya was waiting for him around the corner of the green house. He rushed past her and she followed him in a hurry. It wouldn't even have occurred to passersby that the running girl with the slight squint was not just Zhenya but Evgenia Ivanovna, a teacher.

Kosta dived into a crooked side street, and disappeared behind the entrance door of a house. He rang the bell at an apartment door and immediately heard a peculiar whining and the scratching of strong, sharp-clawed paws on the other side of the door. Then the whining turned into impatient barking, and the scratching into a drumming.

"Quiet, Arty. Wait a minute!" cried Kosta.

The door opened and a light brown dog rushed at Kosta, put his paws on his shoulders, and started licking his nose, eyes, and chin with a long pink tongue.

"Stop it, Arty!"

But the dog wouldn't obey. Zhenya heard a clattering noise as boy and dog went headlong down the staircase. They would have knocked her off her feet had she not pressed herself against the railing. Neither of them paid any attention to her. Arty was running around the yard. He spread his front legs and kicked up his hind legs, like a young goat. He barked, jumped, and kept trying to lick Kosta on his cheek or nose. They ran and played like this, overtaking each other. And then they reluctantly went home.

A thin man on crutches met them at the door. The dog rubbed himself against his solitary leg. The setter's long, soft ears looked a bit like a fur hat with earflaps, with strings missing.

"We've had our walk for today. See you tomorrow," said Kosta.

"Thank you! See you tomorrow."

After Arty disappeared inside it became darker on the landing, as if a bonfire had been put out.

Now they had to go at a run past three blocks of buildings as far as the two-story house with a balcony at the far end of the yard. There was a dog on the balcony, a boxer, with a ferocious mug and a short stump of a tail. He stood on his hind legs with his front ones on the railing. The boxer looked fixedly at the gates of the yard. And when Kosta appeared at the gates, the dog's eyes lit up with sombre joy.

"Attila!" cried Kosta, running into the yard.

The boxer yelped softly, out of sheer happiness.

Kosta ran to the shed, got a ladder and carried it to the balcony. The ladder was heavy and it took the boy quite an effort to lift it. Zhenya could hardly restrain herself from rushing to help him. When Kosta managed to lean the ladder against the balcony, the boxer climbed down into the yard. While rubbing against the boy's trouser legs he kept drawing up one paw; it was evidently hurt.

Kosta produced the food wrapped in a newspaper. The boxer was hungry. He ate greedily, looking at the boy from time to time, and his eyes were brimming with so much feeling that he seemed to be just about to start speaking.

When the dog had finished his lunch, Kosta patted him on the back, fastened a lead to his collar, and they went for a walk. The drooping ends of the dog's big, black-lipped mouth wobbled with each step. Occasionally the dog would draw up his sore paw.

Zhenya heard the janitor woman looking after him say:

"They put the dog on the balcony and went away. And what is there for him to do but die of hunger? Is that human?"

When the walk was over and Kosta was leaving, the dog with his puckered mug and a deep wrinkle on the forehead followed him with eyes full of utter devotion. He wagged his stumpy tail stiffly. Zhenya felt a strong urge to stay with the dog. But Kosta hurried on. In the neighboring house lived an invalid boy on the ground floor; he was bedridden. It was he who owned the dachshund, a black chunk of burnt wood on four legs. Zhenya stood near the window and heard Kosta's conversation with the cripple.

"He's waiting for you," said the boy.

"You just lie down, and don't worry," Kosta told him.

"I'm lying down . . . and I'm not worrying," answered the boy. "Maybe I'll give you my bike if I won't be able to ride it."

"I don't want a bike."

"Mother wants to sell Bootie. She has no time to walk him in the morning."

"I'll come in the morning then," said Kosta after a pause. "Only it will have to be early, before school."

"Won't you have trouble at home?"

"It's all right . . . I'm managing at school . . . just about . . . Only I feel sleepy all the time. I finish my homework late. But you just lie down. Don't worry. Let's go, Bootie!"

So the dachshund was called Bootie. Kosta came out, holding the dog under his arm. And soon they were walking along the pavement. Black Bootie was mincing on his short crooked legs among boots, shoes, moccasins . . . .

Zhenya followed the dachshund, and she had the impression that the big, brown dog had burnt out and turned into this scorched-looking thing. She wished she could talk to Kosta, ask him about the dogs he fed, walked and helped to keep faith in the human race. But she silently followed her pupil who yawned so disgracefully in class and who was so sparing with words. Now he was transformed under her very eyes, like that bunch of wild rosemary.

Bootie had his walk and came back home. Kosta went on, and his invisible companion–Zhenya–again followed him, hiding behind passersby. The houses became smaller and passersby fewer. They were in the outskirts of the town now; here was the start of the dunes. Zhenya could hardly walk on her heels on the loose sand and crooked pine roots. It wasn't long before she broke her heel.

Then she saw the sea.

It was shallow and level. The waves did not fall crashing onto the low shore but crawled up the sand quietly and unhurriedly and then rolled back slowly and noiselessly, leaving a white fringe of foam on the sand. The sea looked sleepy and sluggish, quite incapable of being stormy.

But the storms came all right. Far from the dunes, beyond the horizon.

Kosta walked along the shore, bending forward against the wind. Zhenya had taken off her shoes; it was easier to walk barefooted but the cold damp sand stung her feet. Fishing nets with bottoms of green bottles for floats were hanging on sticks along the shore to dry; overturned boats were lying everywhere.

Suddenly she saw a dog in the distance, at the very edge of the sea, standing motionless, as if in a trance; big-headed, with sharp shoulder blades and a drooping tail, waiting for someone to come back from the sea. Kosta came up to the dog but it didn't even turn its head, as if it didn't hear him coming. He stroked the dog's tangled hair, and the dog moved its tail slightly. The boy squatted down and laid the bread and the remains of his lunch wrapped in a newspaper in front of the dog.

The dog didn't react at all, showed no interest in the food. Kosta began caressing the dog and urging it to eat.

"You must have something to eat . . . Please."

Kosta put a piece of bread up to the dog's mouth.

The dog sighed deeply and noisily and started chewing the bread, slowly eating without gusto, as if it wasn't hungry or was accustomed to better food than plain bread, cold porridge and a piece of tough boiled meat. It ate to stay alive, for it was waiting for someone to come back from the sea.

When the dog finished the food Kosta said:

"Let's go for a walk."

The dog looked at the boy again and followed him obediently. It had heavy paws and an unhurried, dignified gait, like a lion's. Its footsteps filled with water.

The surface of the sea was iridescent with oil slicks, as if a rainbow had broken into pieces as a result of some catastrophe out there beyond the horizon, and the waves had brought its broken pieces to the shore.

The boy and the dog walked slowly, and Zhenya–still following some distance behind–heard the boy say to the dog:

"You are a good dog . . . You are faithful. Come along with me. He will never come back. He is dead. Word of honor."

The dog didn't answer. It simply couldn't. Its eyes were glued to the sea, it didn't believe Kosta. The dog was waiting.

"What am I to do with you?" asked the boy. "You can't live all alone on the shore. You'll have to leave here sooner or later."

The fishing nets ended and Zhenya came into the open as if disentangling herself.

Kosta looked round and saw his teacher. She was standing barefooted on the sand carrying her shoes under her arm. A light wind from the sea tossed her ponytail.

"What is to be done with this dog?" she asked Kosta, dismayed.

"It won't go with me, I know," said the boy. For some reason he was not surprised to see his teacher there. "It will never believe that its master is dead."

Zhenya drew close to the dog, who gave a low growl but didn't bark or attack her.

"I've made a kennel out of an old boat for him. I bring him food. He is so skinny . . . At first he bit me."

"Bit you?"

"Yes, on the hand. It's all right now. I put iodine on it."

They walked a bit further and he said: "Dogs always wait, even for masters who have died. They have to be helped."

The sea became dull in color and seemed to have shrunk. The darkening sky pressed closer to the sleepy waves. Kosta and Zhenya accompanied the dog to its permanent post where an overturned boat lay near the edge of the sea, propped up with a piece of wood so that the dog could crawl under it. The dog went up to the sea, sat on the sand . . .

Next day Kosta fell asleep at the end of the last lesson. He kept yawning, then dropped his head on his arms and fell asleep. At first nobody noticed anything, then somebody giggled, seeing that Kosta was asleep.

"Quiet!" Zhenya said. "Keep quiet!" When she really meant it she could manage them all right. When she said "quiet!" it was quiet.

"Do you know why he fell asleep?" she asked the class in a whisper. "I'll tell you. He walks other people's dogs. He brings them food. Dogs always wait, even for masters who have died. They need to be helped."

The bell rang for the end of the last lesson. It was loud and prolonged, but Kosta didn't hear it. He was sound asleep.

Evgenia Ivanovna, Zhenya, bent over the sleeping boy, put her hand on his shoulder and shook him gently. He started and opened his eyes.

"End of the last lesson. Time for you to go."

Kosta jumped from his seat, grabbed his bag, and the next moment he was gone.

Translated by Margaret Tate

Yuri Yakovlev

Yuri Yakovlev was born in 1922 in Leningrad. He graduated in 1951 from the Gorky Literary Institute in Moscow and was first published in 1947. He is the author of many collections of poems, books of short stories, and novels for children and young people, the most popular of which are: The Railway Station; The Boys; The First Bastilia; Marsh Tea; He Was Quite a Trumpeter, *and* We Are Destined to Live. *He is Founder of the Samantha Project in the USSR, and author of a biography of Samantha Smith, honoring her commitment to peace.*

BULLET

Cynthia Voigt

BULLET HOOKED school the next day: he just got off the bus and went his own way. The thick, triple story of brick waited like a prison, and he didn't go in. Nobody could make him. They could, he guessed, capture him and drag him inside, if they could get a rope onto him—which he doubted.

Anyway, the question never arose. Hanging on to his lunch bag, he moved around the building and down to the playing fields. A couple of first-period gym classes were doing calisthenics, but he went on by them. Nobody asked him any questions. If anybody had, he wouldn't have answered, and if they'd come chasing after him he wouldn't have run. Nobody was going to make him run.

At the oval track he put down his lunch bag and stripped off his sweater and jeans. He folded them into a little pile, the bright red sweater on the brown earth. It was chilly, but the sun was already burning off the morning mist, and the day would grow warm. He ran the cross-country course, ran it five times, ran it hard. Nobody was going to stop him from running.

When the sweat on his chest had dried, he put on his shirt and tied the sweater around his waist by its arms. He walked along down into town, following the main street right up to where it ended at the water. Then he followed the water around to Patrice's, going through shallows when there was no public pathway. By the time he got out there, his sneakers were sodden and muddy and his jeans clung to his calves.

Patrice wasn't home. His truck was gone. Bullet went out and sat on the deck of *Fraternité* for a while. He would have hosed her down except she was always kept clean. He ate his sandwiches, then went along the dock to drop the crumpled-up bag into Patrice's incinerator. He hung around the yard for a while, seeing what Patrice was up to. The fourteen-footer was almost finished. The ribs were in and boards ran its entire curved length–fitted so neatly you almost couldn't see that it was made of separate boards. A new transom lay nearby, needing sanding before it could be set into place, the joints cut out like pieces of a jigsaw puzzle. Bullet ran his hand along the sides of the boat, sanded to silky smoothness, ready for an undercoat. He didn't know how Patrice stood it, all that slow work, but he surely admired the results, and even admired Patrice for being able to achieve them.

He turned and looked around the yard. A couple of hulls, an empty boat trailer digging its nose into the ground, motors and propellers. Then he stepped over the picket fence.

The road by Patrice's was lined on both sides with little houses, each house surrounded by a yard and fence. The other yards, past which Bullet jogged, were planted and tended, kept neat. It bothered his neighbors that Patrice didn't plant and tend his lawn. Every now and then, somebody would write him a note, anonymous, of course, or a group of men would come to try to talk to him about keeping up the neighborhood. Patrice never minded them, but it made Bullet mad, and these little boxed-in gussied-up yards didn't show him anything either.

His return route took him through one of the colored sections. Not the higher income one, that was downtown. This was shacks along the roadside, built from tar paper over cinderblock footings; or old trailers with patches of vegetable gardens beside them; or once even an old bus, with a bedspread hung for a door. Bullet jogged past the section fast; it made him angry.

He arrived home mid-afternoon and went right upstairs to get his gun. He stopped in the kitchen for a couple of glasses of milk, which he drank standing up, looking out the window over the sink. He could see his mother off around the corner, checking the sheets on the clothesline. They weren't dry yet, but a late afternoon breeze was building up and that would probably finish the job. The cool milk flowed down his throat.

He heard heavy footsteps behind him, the old man. He didn't turn around, didn't hurry himself. He felt the old man's anger wash over him from behind and almost smiled. Slowly, he lifted the glass to empty it. Slowly, he turned on water, rinsed the glass, set it down slowly on the washboard. He wondered what the old man would do if he turned around to face him. He'd said he didn't want to lay eyes on Bullet. What would he do if Bullet turned around?. . . Run out of the room?

Bullet turned around.

His father was staring at the toes of his shoes and his eyes didn't even flicker, so Bullet knew the man had been staring at them all the time he'd been standing there. He could have laughed.

"There is nothing quite so childish as getting even by wanton destruction," the old man said to his shoes.

Bullet wondered what would happen if ten little voices answered back: "Yes sir . . . yes sir . . . yes sir," overlapping one another like waves coming into shore. He stared at his father's bent head, to where the face began, under the white crown. He stared hard, wanting to force the guy to look up and eat his own words.

"You'll repair the damage you did."

I did what I was told. They close now–I checked that.

"They'll need to be completely rebuilt now."

So what?

"Then rehung. On new hinges." The orders came marching out. "You'll have to rebuild the frame first."

You can't make me.

"If not right away, you'll have to do it sooner or later, whenever–"

Bullet knew what he was about to get to. *Unh-uh, you're not going to do that to me.*

"When it's yours."

You can't make me.

"So that you have succeeded only in fouling your own nest. Like any other animal, like some nigger. I am not surprised at that, not surprised at all."

–not going to hang that around my neck. Box me in with it. Use it that way. Take it away from me. Because nothing felt under his feet the way the rich, flat acres of home did.

"Because the farm is yours, or as good as. Not that I particularly want to give it to you."

You don't want to give it to anyone, you want to pull it into your grave after you like some blanket.

"And I hope it chokes you like it's choked me."

Anger burned up in Bullet's guts and his bones closed in around it. He got his hands on his gun and got out of the room. His father wanted to make Bullet take it from him because he hated it; he couldn't make Bullet take anything from him. Nobody could do that, but nobody. They kept trying to box him in, and he kept breaking out–and he'd keep on breaking out, damn them.

He went around behind the barn and into a thin patch of woods. He moved fast, and his noisy progress routed two crows out of the branches. Without thinking, he shouldered, cocked, aimed the gun and fired twice. He got one. Not bad. Even with the second-rate gun, his marksmanship was OK, maybe even good. When he could pick up the Smith and Wesson in Salisbury, he'd be good enough for it.

Bullet slowed down, moving more quietly. In another couple of weeks the hunting season would begin, and he'd have to get himself a bright orange hat. But now he didn't have to worry about being picked off by some jerk from some city who mistook him for a deer, or maybe a duck. He thought, sliding the clip into place and shoving the bolt home, if he saw some ducks he might shoot for them. Game wardens stayed home as long as they could, earning their salaries by shuffling papers on a desk until they had to get out into the cold to actually keep an eye on things. It wasn't even cold yet, just crisp in the shady woods. If he flushed any ducks and was close enough, he might just shoot for them. Who'd see him here? Who could catch him?

All of his senses alert, he walked the woods and fields as the afternoon gathered in around him. Once he got a shot at a rabbit, off to the left inlaid, but he missed. He opened the bolt, picked up the empty casing and jammed it into his pocket, then slid the bolt home again, hearing the bullet click into place. For a while, he sat in a clearing, just in case a deer might come browsing by near enough to justify trying for it. Across the open space, the bare trees rose into a gray sky, each branch clear. A breeze flowed along the land, running for the water. It soughed through the pines, and the top-heavy loblollies swayed under its hands. No deer came by.

When Bullet moved back into the woods, it was twilight there, darker than in the open, the light dim and shadowy. He stopped, pulled his sweater over his head, and then–holding the twenty-two ready, like a pistol at his right hip–he tossed a couple of dead branches up into a pine, seeing if anything flushed out. Nothing moved.

But something moved off to his right, low and on the ground, at the edge of his vision . . . He got the shot off before he even properly saw, a sweet reflex shot, his whole body coordinated and working like a perfect machine.

A good shot too, he heard the cry and the muffled thud of a small body falling to ground in mid-movement. His hands worked the bolt to reload the barrel automatically as he went over to the bushes to see what he'd gotten.

OD–the stupid mutt–lay on her side with blood coming out every time she breathed. Her eyes were closed.

Bullet knew what he had to do next. He raised the gun to his shoulder and aimed just behind her left eye. At this range, even this gun wouldn't fail him. "I *told* you," he said to her. He hooked his finger around the trigger. He wanted to do this in one clean shot. Why did she have to be so stupid?

At the sound of his voice she opened her eye and her tail wagged a couple of times. It barely rustled the leaves and branches she lay on.

"You stupid mutt," Bullet said. "What am I supposed to do?"

The tail moved again, and she tried to lift her head to see him, but apparently she couldn't.

Bullet crouched down beside her and took a look at the wound. It was a kind of ragged hole in her rib cage. She tried to turn, tried to get up–her front legs kind of scrabbled and her chest heaved; her back legs didn't move at all. Blood came out of the hole, slow and steady.

"What did you think you were doing?" he demanded. But she hadn't been thinking, and now look what had happened. She'd just been following him around and got in the wrong place at the wrong time. Stupid, just like Liza, and wagging her tail at him when he'd just pumped lead into her.

Bullet forced his rib cage outward with a breath.

Not his fault, he knew that.

His rib cage and the banded muscles of his diaphragm closed in again, putting pressure on his lungs.

She walked into it. Time and again, over and over, he'd sent her home. The stupid dog just wouldn't learn.

He forced breath into his lungs.

He felt like kicking her. It made him angry . . . what she'd done. His muscles bunched together and moved with anger. He rose, bent to pick up the twenty-two, stared down at the dog making a puddle of dark blood on the dried pine needles.

She lay there uncomplaining, breathing, bleeding–dying.

It wasn't his fault, but he had fired the shot. And now what was he supposed to do. He felt boxed in, helpless–caught in somebody else's trap, like always. He needed to yell, he needed to move, before the sides of the box pushed in all around him and crushed him.

He felt himself explode into action, swinging his arms–and he cracked the twenty-two against the twisted trunk of a swamp oak. The shock of the impact ran along his bones, jarring the shoulder socket and moving on, like a lightning bolt, down through the muscles of his back. He slammed it again and again. The noise he was making with his voice had no meaning, it just exploded out of him.

At last, the gun broke, snapped apart where the barrel joined the stock. The barrel flew off into the dark woods, landing with a crash. He threw the stock after it, listening to it fly through branches and crash down somewhere in the dark circle beyond visibility.

He was breathing heavily. He turned to look down at OD before walking away.

Her ears were up, listening. She didn't even know what was going on.

Bullet sat down on the rough ground by her head. "All right," he said aloud. "But hurry up." He put one hand on her head, rubbing a little with his fingers. He could feel the shape of her skull under the smooth hair. Her skull fit into his hand. If he wanted to, he could take his two hands and crush that circle of bone–if she'd been in pain he would have. His fingers moved behind her floppy ear. Along the edge of the delicate layer of bone.

She was small, OD, smaller even than that kid in the picture

Frank showed him. Liza's kid. He didn't believe Liza had gone and had a kid, with Frank for the father–and maybe two. How stupid could anyone be.

You're not looking too smart to me right now, he told himself.

It wasn't my fault, he answered.

Yeah, but it's your responsibility.

Well, I'm accepting that, so shut up.

He shut up.

OD breathed slowly, patiently, waiting. Bullet breathed beside her, waiting. Night settled slowly in around them, sifting in among the trees. She wasn't complaining, OD. She wasn't scared. Little night noises moved around them, scurryings and flutterings, the rustling of leaves and sometimes a distant motor, some boat moving back to harbor.

Bullet felt the hard ground under his backside and his legs. His shoulders rested back against a fallen tree. His one hand rested on OD's skull, the little finger going down along her neck to register the shallow rise and fall of her breathing.

He sat between anger and sadness. They felt the same, the sadness and the anger. He could see the shapes of trees and the massy shape of undergrowth, but nothing more. He could see, turning his head slightly, the whitish shape of OD.

"I'm sorry, OD," he finally spoke aloud. He barely recognized his own voice. He heard a rustle of dried pine needles where her tail was. "I dunno, I wish you hadn't walked into it. I wish I hadn't taken that shot–I didn't mean to."

If she knew anything, which he doubted, she'd know that was true. Which didn't make any difference. "You're such a stupid mutt, OD," his voice said, trying to tell her, "but you've been OK." And she couldn't possibly understand, he knew that. "You've been an OK dog, all things considered."

Shut up, he told himself.

Well, she was.

Night folded in over them. The wind picked up, and he could no longer hear OD's breathing. He could only feel it through his fingers. The moon must have risen, because the woods was infiltrated with silvery clouds of light that made patches of dark shadows. The shadows moved, where they ran through trees. The wind washed cold over Bullet. He didn't move. He stayed and waited. He had no idea how much time passed and he didn't care. And then, quietly, OD was no longer breathing. Because he had killed her.

He got up, stiff and angry. But he was angry at himself. He didn't know what to do about that.

Johnny was right, you're a breaker, he told himself. *She had courage. She was nothing but a stupid mutt, and she did it right. Good for you,* OD.

In the shadowy woods, there wasn't anything he could dig a grave with. He started digging with his fingers where he'd been sitting, but after the layer of dead needles and dried leaves scraped off, and the top dusty layer of soil, all he could do was scratch uselessly. He felt around until he found a stick, strong enough. He used that to scrape and pry and dig into the soil. With his hands, he scooped out the handfuls of soil he loosened that way and piled it by his knees. Then he scraped and pried again.

After a long time, he had made a shallow grave. He picked up the body of the dog–just a body now, empty–and put her into it. Scraping with his hands, he covered her over with dirt. After the dirt, he piled on armloads of leaves, and finally, with the heaviest branches he could find, he made a covering. He set the branches side by side in a straight row over the grave.

He stood up, cold and stiff, but not tired. *That was such a stupid thing to do. A stupid mistake. Mine.*

Bullet made his way down to the water and went north toward the farm. Along by the water the sky showed stars and moon overhead. Liza should have taken OD with her. Liza knew what it was like. Leaving OD there was like—Bullet splashed up through the cold shallows. It was like lions, the way the old man—and he did it too—devoured things. Like lions attacking and chasing down, teeth and claws and the powerful relentless bodies. Then ripping her apart, ripping the flesh and bones apart, and the blood, guts, everything lying on the ground. . . . Poor OD didn't have a chance, nobody could have stopped them.

Come off it, he said to himself. *What kind of an idea is that?*

It's just an idea, he answered, *but it's my own, and maybe even the first one all my own. So get lost.*

Get lost (scornfully), *how can I get lost? Jerk.*

Bullet agreed.

He turned at the dock, to go inland. Over the marsh grasses the sky lightened to silver, and a streak of orangy pink heralded the sunrise. Bullet stopped to watch. He wasn't in any hurry.

As the light rose above a line of trees, it flowed like water over the grasses, turning them warm brown, almost gold. They swayed, as if the light were a hand passing over them. The distant trees assumed color.

Bullet headed up the path. He came through the pines into his mother's vegetable garden. There the brown harrowed earth shone under early sunlight, and the few dark leaves hanging on the tomato plants glowed. A couple of pumpkins were hidden away under broad flat leaves, their vines twisting along the rough earth. Tiny tentacles went out from the vines to hold the soil. He bent down and took a handful of dirt, rubbing it with his fingers against his palm, letting it shower down. You grew things out of this, and his fingers could feel its richness.

He looked toward the house and met his mother's eyes. She was sitting on the back steps, still in the clothes she'd worn for dinner, red shoes with heels, blue skirt, the white blouse. He walked toward her. Her hands held a blanket around her shoulders. Her eyes were fixed on his face. She had been waiting for him.

"Maw," he said.

She didn't answer. Her face stayed expressionless.

"What are you *doing?*" he demanded.

"You took your gun," she snapped.

He turned, looked where she was looking, over the garden to the marsh. He sat down beside her, so his shoulder almost touched hers. He could feel how she was feeling, and he didn't like feeling that; he didn't like her feeling it either; it made him angry that she should have to.

With his shoulder touching hers, he tried to tell her. "I shot OD." He waited, and she didn't say anything. "It was an accident. Anyway, I waited with her–and then I had to bury her."

The two of them sat looking out. He waited for what she would answer. He wouldn't blame her if she let fly at him.

"People like us," she finally said, "I dunno, boy. Innocent, weak things come into our hands, and we do such a bad job by them. We destroy them."

"It wasn't like that; it was an accident," he told her.

She turned her head to face him, her eyes burning. "Don't pretend, boy. Are you pretending to yourself you didn't do it? Because if you are, you're lying to yourself. Are you doing that? Are you going to do that to yourself?"

Her anger drove the breath out of him, and he pulled his body back from hers. "But," he started to say, and her mouth moved without saying anything. She wasn't talking to him, he understood that; he understood her anger.

"No, I'm not," he promised her. Her head nodded once, sharply. *What a life for her,* he suddenly thought, angry and sad again. *Why didn't she get out, why doesn't she?*

"You don't know," she said.

"No, I don't think I do," he told her. Then a sudden question drove everything else out of his head.

"Do you think I should have carried her home? Do you think a vet could have done anything? Momma?"

She asked him to describe the wound, so he did, his answers as quiet as her questions. He didn't try to explain how it happened, just talked about what OD looked like. His mother thought about it, then shook her head. "No, bringing her home wouldn't have been any good."

Bullet believed her, but he couldn't be sure.

"Besides, we'd have had to sail into town to find a vet," his mother said.

"And I wouldn't have liked to bury her in the water," Bullet said.

"Agreed."

They sat in silence. She was cold, he realized. "You should go inside," he said.

"I am tired, I am that." But she didn't get up. "And my feet hurt."

"Take off your shoes. Why didn't you take off your shoes?"

"And ruin a pair of perfectly good stockings?"

"Take off your stockings too."

"Bare feet are common," she reminded him.

"You don't think that," he told her. *Talk about boxes.*

She didn't answer. He guessed he knew why.

"Maw?" he said. "You're the stubbornest old woman in the world."

A smile moved across her face and was gone. Watching that, Bullet thought: *How long has it been? What a life for her,* and then, loud inside his own head, *I won't let him do this to her.*

And what are you going to do? he asked himself. *What can you do?*

Something.

You're the breaker. You destroy. You forgotten already?

No. No, I haven't.

He thought maybe he could tell her about Frank's visit, just about the picture of the kid. But then he recognized that that wouldn't be much joy to her, finding out she had a grandchild, and maybe two, that she didn't even know where they were and wouldn't be able to get off the farm to go find them even if she wanted to. That would just be adding more boards to the side of her box, making her box squeeze tighter on her. It would be like turning her into prey, sticking his lion's claws and teeth into her. He couldn't get her out of her box any more than he could unshoot the shot that got OD. There was nothing he could do.

Everybody was in the same box, helpless. She was and he was–and maybe even the old man, although Bullet couldn't see that, but maybe she could–and everybody. *What a world.*

"I don't recall any orders about me cooking for you, do you?" Bullet asked his mother. He stood up. She looked at him.

"You used to have a sense of humor," she told him. Her hair, streaked with gray, hung in a braid down her back.

Bullet couldn't make any sense out of that remark. He wondered if he'd been wrong about her, overestimated her strength.

"A good one," she said, thoughtfully.

"I still do," Bullet told her and wondered if she was cracking up, had been cracking, slowly, over the years, while they–him and the old man–lionlike devoured her.

She snorted. "You could fool me."

Then Bullet saw what she meant and did smile. "I doubt that–I never could fool you. I've got eggs and some bacon. I fry me a mean egg. We could eat standing up." He wanted to give her something, even just breakfast.

She shook her head. "No. No I can't do that."

Anger rose up in Bullet again, and again sadness. "Stubborn," he told her, "stubborn *and* proud. I dunno, Maw, you're gonna get yourself into trouble."

That brought another smile to her face, a sudden smile, as suddenly gone. She knew what he was thinking. "You, boy," she said.

He left her there on the back steps, with her face turned to the garden, the marsh, and if she could have seen beyond it, the water.

Cynthia Voigt

Cynthia Voigt was born in 1942 in Boston, Massachusetts. She was raised in Connecticut and was a graduate of Dana Hall School and Smith College in Massachusetts. For a number of years she taught English and the classics. Cynthia Voigt's first novel, Homecoming, *was nominated for the American Book Award.* Dicey's Song, *a sequel to* Homecoming, *won the Newbery Medal. She has also written* Tell Me If the Lovers Are Losers, The Callender Papers, *and* A Solitary Blue. *She lives in Annapolis, Maryland, with her husband, their two children, and the family dog.*

QUIET MORNING

Yuri Kazakov

YASHA WOKE up when sleepy roosters were just beginning to crow, the house still stood in darkness, Mother had not yet milked the cow nor the shepherd taken the herd out into the meadows.

The boy sat up on his bed and stared for quite a while at the bluish misty windows and the hazy whiteness of the stove. Slumber is sweet before dawn. His head toppled back onto the pillow and he could hardly keep his eyes open, but he took hold of himself. Stumbling and clutching at benches and chairs, he began groping around the house, looking for his old trousers and shirt.

He had some milk and bread, took his fishing rods from the entrance hall and stepped out onto the porch. The village was covered with a huge eiderdown of fog. The nearby houses were still visible, but those further away were just dark splotches and you couldn't see anything at all down by the river. It seemed as if there had never been any windmill on the hill; no fire tower, no school, and no forest on the horizon. Everything had vanished, was hidden now so that Yasha's house became the center of that small closed world.

Somebody had been up before Yasha and was now hammering by the smithy; pure metallic sounds tore through the veil of fog, reached the invisible big barn and came back smothered. It seemed as if two people were hammering, one loudly and the other softly.

Yasha hopped down the porch, swung his rods at a rooster which had got in his way, and blithely trotted toward the threshing barn. There he fetched a rusty chopper from under a board and began to dig. He came across cold purple and lilac worms almost right away. Thick or thin, they were equally swift to burrow into the mellow earth, but Yasha still managed to snatch them and soon had nearly a tinful. He sprinkled the worms with a bit of fresh earth and rushed down a path, tumbled over a fence and on through backyards toward the shed, in which his new pal, Volodya, was sleeping in the hayloft.

Yasha thrust his earth-smeared fingers into his mouth and whistled. Then he spat out and listened. Everything was quiet.

"Volodya!" he called out. "Get up!"

Volodya stirred in the hay, dawdled and rustled there for quite a while, and finally climbed down awkwardly, stepping on his untied shoelaces. His face, crumpled with sleep, was blank and immobile, like the face of a blind person, bits of hay were stuck in his hair and some must have got under his shirt, too, because when he was down and standing by Yasha, he kept on jerking his thin neck, shrugging his shoulders and scratching his back.

"Isn't it a bit early?" he asked huskily, yawned, lurched, and steadied himself against the ladder.

Yasha got furious. He had got up an hour earlier, dug up the worms, brought the rods . . . and, to tell the truth, had got up today especially for this wretch–had wanted to show him the fishing grounds–and all he got instead of thanks and admiration was that "a bit early"!

"It may be a bit early for you!" he said savagely and eyed Volodya from head to toe with contempt.

Volodya peeped out into the street, his face livened up, his eyes sparkled and he began hastily to lace up his shoes. But for Yasha the charm of the early morning was already ruined.

"What's wrong with you? Are you going to wear shoes?" he asked disdainfully and looked at the sticking toe of his bare foot. "And how about a pair of galoshes?"

Volodya didn't answer, just blushed and started doing up the other shoe.

"Why, of course," Yasha went on gloomily, leaning the rods against the wall, "none of you walk barefoot in Moscow . . ."

"So what?" Volodya looked up at Yasha's broad, maliciously-mocking face.

"Nothing . . . Why not drop by your place to fetch a coat?"

"So I will!" Volodya muttered through his clenched teeth and blushed even more.

Yasha felt bored. He wished he hadn't gone to all that trouble. Even Kolya and Zhenya Voronkov, crack anglers as they were, admitted that he was as good an angler as anybody in the village. If he were to show them just one good fishing spot, he'd be showered with apples! While this one here . . . came yesterday, all sweet talk: "Will you, please" . . . Shall I knock the daylights out of him or what? I wish I'd had nothing to do with this Muscovite who has probably never seen a live fish in his life! Going fishing with his shoes on! The idea!

"You better put your tie on," Yasha taunted him and gave a gruff laugh. "Fish take offense here if you come along without a tie."

Volodya had at last coped with his shoes and went out of the shed, his nostrils quivering with resentment, eyes gazing straight ahead. He was ready to call off the fishing and to burst into tears there and then but he had been looking forward to this morning so much! Yasha reluctantly followed him out and they started walking down the street in silence, not looking at each other. They walked through the village and the fog kept retreating in front of them, revealing ever new houses, sheds, the school and long rows of milk-white farm buildings. Like a close-fisted host, it showed everything, but only for a minute and again closed tightly behind them.

Volodya was suffering dismally. He was angry with himself for his rude answers to Yasha, angry with Yasha, and thought he looked clumsy and miserable. He was ashamed of his clumsiness and, to deaden that unpleasant feeling, reflected bitterly: "All right, let him . . . Let him make fun of me! They'll hear of me one day, I won't let them make a butt of me! Look at him walking barefoot! Just showing off!" At the same time he glanced with frank envy and even admiration at Yasha's bare feet, sackcloth fish bag, patched trousers and grey shirt worn specially for fishing. He also envied Yasha's suntan and that strange way of walking that made the shoulders, shoulder blades and even the ears move, which was considered smart by many village boys. They reached a well with an old log frame overgrown with green moss.

"Stop!" Yasha said glumly. "Let's have a drink!"

He went up to the well, rattled the chain, pulled up a heavy wooden bucket of water and began to drink it greedily. He wasn't thirsty but believed that there was nothing like that water and for this reason drank it with relish every time he passed by the well. Water splashed from the bucket onto his bare feet, he tucked them out of the way but went on drinking, tearing himself away from the bucket from time to time and breathing noisily.

"Here, drink!" he told Volodya, wiping his mouth on a sleeve.

Volodya wasn't thirsty either but obediently pressed his mouth to the rim, so as not to make Yasha even more cross, and began sipping water until his head ached from the cold.

"How d'you like it?" Yasha queried complacently when Volodya had stepped away from the well.

"Just swell!" Volodya rejoined, shivering.

"I'll bet there's nothing like it in Moscow!" Yasha screwed up his eyes with a challenge.

Volodya said nothing but only sucked in the air through his clenched teeth and gave a conciliatory smile.

"Have you ever been fishing?" Yasha asked.

"No, but I've seen people fish in the Moskva River," Volodya said weakly and cast a shy glance at Yasha.

This confession placated Yasha, who touched the worm tin and said casually:

"Yesterday our club-house director saw a sheatfish in the Pleshansky pool."

"A big one?" Volodya's eyes glowed.

"Sure! About two metres long . . . perhaps even three: he couldn't quite see it in the dark. He even got scared–thought it was a crocodile. Believe it or not!"

"It can't be true!" Volodya breathed out in raptures and shrugged his shoulders; his eyes showed that he believed every word of it without reservation.

"Can't be true?" Yasha exclaimed in astonishment. "Let's go fishing tonight if you like! What d'you say?"

"Could we?" Volodya gave voice to his hope, his ears going pink.

"Why not?" Yasha spat and wiped his nose on a sleeve. "I've got the tackle. We'll catch frogs and loaches . . . Take dew-worms for bait–there's chubfish there, too–and we'll stay overnight. We'll make a fire . . . Coming?"

Volodya felt wild with happiness and it was not until then that he had realized how much he enjoyed walking out-of-doors in the morning. How good and easy it was to breathe, what an urge he had to run upon that soft road, to go full speed, jumping and squealing with delight!

What was it tinkling strangely there behind them? What was it that suddenly cried out in the meadow, distinctly and melodiously, as if striking a taut string several times? Where had this already happened to him? Or perhaps it hadn't? But why then was that feeling of delight and happiness so familiar?

What was it that crackled so loudly in the field? A motorcycle? Volodya looked inquiringly at Yasha.

"It's a tractor!" Yasha said with an air of importance.

"A tractor? Why is it crackling then?"

"The engine is being started. It'll catch soon . . . Listen, hear it? Now it's droning! Bound to go on now . . . It's Fedya Kostylev. He was ploughing all night with the headlights on, then slept for a while, and now he's back at work again."

Volodya looked in the direction of the droning tractor and immediately asked: "D'you always have fog like this?"

"No. Sometimes it's clear and sometimes–later, closer to September–hoar-frost can fall, all of a sudden. But in general fish take the bait better when it's foggy–you just pull them out!"

"What sort of fish d'you have?"

"Why, all sorts. There is crucian on some stretches of the river, pike and, well . . . perch, roach, bream . . . and also tench. You know what tench is, don't you? Fa-a-t like a piglet! My mouth fell open when I first caught one myself."

"Can you catch a lot here?"

"H'm . . . It depends. Sometimes up to five kilograms and then sometimes only enough for a cat."

"What's the whistle?" Volodya paused and raised his head.

"The whistle? It's wee ducks . . . little she-teals."

"Aha, I know . . . and what's that other sound?"

"It's thrushes singing. They've come to Auntie Nastya's garden for some rowan. Have you ever caught thrushes?"

"Never."

"Mishka Kayunenok has a net. Just you wait and we'll go after them. Thrushes, they are greedy devils, flying in flocks over the fields and snatching worms from under the tractors. All you have to do is spread a net, throw about some rowan, then take cover and wait. When they come, at least five at a time would try to get under the net. They're rather funny; not all of them, of course, but some are real smart. One winter I kept a thrush that hummed like a locomotive and screeched like a saw."

The village was soon left behind. Fields of dwarfish oats stretched on and on, and a dark strip of woods could barely be discerned ahead.

"Is it still a long way to go?" Volodya asked now and then.

"Soon be there . . . It's quite close. Let's walk a bit faster," Yasha answered every time.

They reached a knoll, turned right, went down a hollow, followed a path through a flax field—and the river came into view all of a sudden.

It was smallish, densely overgrown with broom and willows along the banks, it rippled over shoals and every now and then expanded into deep and gloomy pools.

The sun had at last risen; a horse whinnied in a meadow, and everything around grew light and pink amazingly swiftly; grey dew became distinctly visible on fir trees and bushes and the fog, beginning to move, dispersed and reluctantly unveiled haystacks, dark against the smokey backdrop of the woods that were now quite close. Fish were jumping.

Heavy splashes occasionally resounded in the pools, the water trembled and the riverside bulrushes swayed softly.

Volodya was ready to begin fishing there and then but Yasha kept pushing ahead along the river bank. They had got wet with dew almost to their waists when Yasha finally whispered, "This is the place!" and began climbing down toward the water. He stumbled inadvertently, dank lumps of earth rolled from under his feet, and instantly invisible ducks quacked, flapped their wings, took off and flew above the river, disappearing in the fog. Yasha stiffened and hissed like a goose. Volodya licked his parched lips and jumped down after Yasha. He looked around and was stunned by the gloom reigning over that pool. It smelled of dampness, clay and slime, the water was black, the riotous willows blotted out the sky almost completely and, even though their tops were already pink with sunlight and the blue sky could be seen through the fog, it was damp, gloomy and cold down there by the river.

"D'you know how deep it is here?" Yasha's eyes swelled. "There's no bottom."

Volodya stepped away from the water and started when a fish splashed with a thud by the opposite bank.

"We never swim in this pool."

"Why?" asked Volodya in a weak voice.

"You can get sucked in. Once your legs are down, it's the end of you. The water is ice cold–and down you go. Mishka Kayunenok says there are octopuses at the bottom."

"Octopuses live only . . . in the sea," Volodya said uncertainly and edged farther away from the water.

" 'In the sea!' . . . I know that! But Mishka saw one. He went fishing and was passing by when he suddenly saw a tentacle shoot out of the water and start groping about the shore . . . Well? Mishka took to his heels and never stopped till he reached the village! But then he might be lying, for all I know," Yasha concluded somewhat unexpectedly and began unwinding the lines.

Volodya cheered up while Yasha, who had already forgotten the octopuses, looked impatiently at the river and every time a fish splashed noisily his face looked painfully strained. He got the tackle ready, passed one rod to Volodya, put some worms into a matchbox for him and indicated with his eyes a place to fish from.

Yasha cast his line and stared impatiently at the float, his rod still in his hand. Almost immediately Volodya, too, threw his line but his rod got caught on a willow. Yasha looked at Volodya furiously, cursed under his breath and when his eyes shifted back to his float all he saw instead were spreading circular ripples. He hooked right away with all his might, smoothly moved his hand to the right, and took pleasure in feeling a fish pull hard as it dived deeply; but suddenly the line went slack and the empty hook popped out of the water. Yasha trembled with fury.

"Got away, did it? Got away," he kept whispering, fixing another worm on the hook with his wet hands.

He cast his line again, and again stared fixedly at the float, waiting for a bite and keeping the rod in his hand. But the fish wouldn't bite and even splashes could no longer be heard. His arm soon grew tired and he carefully stuck the rod into the soft bank. Volodya looked at Yasha and also stuck his rod in.

Rising higher and higher, the sun at last peeped into that gloomy pool. The water instantly twinkled dazzlingly, and dew-drops glowed on leaves, grass and flowers. Volodya blinked at his float, then turned and asked uncertainly: "Can a fish move off to another pool?"

"Of course it can!" Yasha replied fiercely. "That one got off and scared the rest of them away. Must be quite big . . . When I pulled I felt quite a tug. Could have been about a kilogram."

Yasha was a little ashamed to have let the fish go but, as often happens, he was inclined to blame Volodya for his failure. "An angler indeed! Sitting there bow-legged. It's always teeming with fish when you're alone or with a true angler." He wanted to sting Volodya in some way but suddenly snatched his rod: the float had twitched slightly. Straining, as if he were trying to uproot a tree, he slowly pulled the rod out of the ground and, holding it suspended, slightly lifted it. The float swung anew, slanted sideways, stayed that way for a while and then straightened again. Yasha took a breath, squinted, and saw Volodya go pale and start rising slowly. Yasha felt hot, small drops of sweat stood out on his nose and upper lip. The float quivered again and moved to one side, half sank and finally disappeared, leaving behind a barely visible swirl of water. Like the other time, Yasha hooked softly and immediately leaned forward, trying to straighten up the rod. The line and the trembling float drew a curve, Yasha rose to his feet, got hold of the rod with the other hand and, feeling powerful and frequent jerks, again gently moved his arms to the right. Volodya jumped toward Yasha, his rounded excited eyes sparkling, and he cried out shrilly: "C'mon, c'mon, c'mo-o-n!"

"Clear off!" Yasha breathed out huskily, backing and shifting his feet rapidly.

For an instant the fish leaped out of the water, showing its broad, glittering side, struck heavily with its tail, raised a pink spray and darted back into the cold depths. Propping the butt-end of the rod against his stomach, Yasha continued backing and crying out: "No, you don't! No, you don't!"

He finally brought the threshing fish closer to the shore, jerked it out onto the grass and fell, stomach down, upon it. Volodya's throat went dry and his heart was beating frantically. "What is it you have there?" he asked, squatting. "Show me what you've got there."

"A bream!" Yasha uttered ecstatically.

He carefully pulled the big cold bream from under him, turned his broad, happy face to Volodya and gave a husky laugh–but his smile went out all of a sudden, his eyes staring in fright at something behind Volodya's back; he tensed and gasped: "Your rod . . . Look!"

Volodya turned and saw that his rod had pushed aside a lump of earth and was slowly slipping into the water, something powerfully tugging the line. He jumped to his feet, stumbled and, stretching out on his knees, managed to seize the rod. It bent sharply and Volodya turned his pale round face toward Yasha.

"Hold on!" Yasha cried out.

But at that moment the earth gave under Volodya's feet, he lost his balance, let go of the rod, awkwardly flung up his arms as if catching a ball, emitted a loud "Ah-a-a!" and fell into the water.

"You fool!" Yasha shouted hoarsely, his face contorted with fury. "You damn fool! You've scared away the fish!"

He jumped to his feet, snatched a lump of turf to hurl into Volodya's face the moment he came to the surface. But when he looked at the water he froze and had that agonizing feeling one usually has in sleep when one's limp body defies one's mind: about three meters away from the shore Volodya was slapping his hands against the water, throwing his white goggle-eyed face toward the sky, choking and going under the water, still straining to cry out something but gurgling instead and uttering, "Whah . . . Whah . . ."

"He's drowning!" Yasha had the terrifying thought. "He's being pulled down!" He dropped the lump of turf and, wiping his sticky hand on his trousers, his eyes still on the other boy feeling his feet go weak, he started backing up the shore away from the river. Mishka's tale about huge octopuses at the bottom of the pool came to his mind and his chest and stomach went cold with horror: it occurred to him that an octopus had caught hold of Volodya. The earth crumbled under his feet and, leaning on his trembling arms, he clumsily struggled uphill.

Spurred on by the horrible sounds coming from Volodya, Yasha at last sprang out into the meadow and sprinted toward the village but hardly had he made a dozen steps when he came to a stop as if stuck, feeling that he couldn't go away. There was nobody around, nobody to turn to for help. He feverishly fumbled in his pockets and bag for a piece of string but found nothing, and white as a sheet, began crawling back to the pool. He reached the cliff and looked down, expecting to see something terrible and at the same time hoping that the matter had settled itself somehow, and again saw Volodya. He no longer struggled and was almost completely under water, only the top of his head with the hair sticking out was still showing. It kept disappearing and coming up, disappearing and coming up again. His eyes riveted to Volodya's head, Yasha started unbuttoning his trousers, then screamed and tumbled down. He threw off his trousers and plunged into water, his shirt still on and the bag across his shoulder, and with two strokes swam up to Volodya and grasped his hand.

Volodya got hold of Yasha right away and quickly ran his fingers up Yasha's arm, clutching at his shirt and bag, thrusting his weight upon Yyasha, and uttering as before that inhuman, terrible sound, "Whah . . . Whah . . ." Water rushed into Yasha's mouth. Feeling the iron grip upon his neck, he tried to push his face up out of the water but Volodya, shivering, kept on thrusting his weight upon him, trying to climb onto his shoulders. Water got into Yasha's lungs, making him cough, choke and swallow more water, and then a wild, incredible terror seized him, and red and yellow circles flared up with a dazzle in his eyes. He realized that Volodya would drown him, that he was breathing his last; he jerked with all his might, struggled and uttering the same inhuman and horrible cry that Volodya had uttered a minute ago, kicked Volodya in the stomach, came to the surface and, through the water running from his hair, saw the bright flat globe of the sun. Still feeling Volodya's weight upon himself, Yasha flung him away, began to whip water with his arms and legs, raising foam waves, and in terror dashed toward the bank.

It was not until he grasped the riverside sedge that he came to his senses and looked back. The troubled water of the pool was calming down and there was already nobody to be seen. Several bubbles of air came up to the surface, and Yasha's teeth began to chatter.

He turned around–the sun was shining brightly, making the leaves of the bushes and willows glisten, an iridescent cobweb shone among the wild flowers, a wagtail on a log above shook its tail and looked at Yasha with its sparkling eye, and everything was as it had always been, peaceful and quiet. It was a quiet morning but something extraordinary had happened just now, not so long ago—a man had drowned and it was he, Yasha, who had struck him and caused him to drown.

Yasha blinked, let go of the sedge, shrugged his shoulders under the wet shirt, inhaled deeply, and dived. When he opened his eyes under water he saw nothing at first; vague yellowish and greenish splotches and some water-weeds were quivering all around, lit by the sun. But the sunlight did not penetrate down into the depths. Yasha went farther down, swam a little, his hands and face touching the water-weeds, and then saw Volodya. He was on his side, one leg entangled in the weeds, slowly turning, rocking, putting his round pale face into the sunlight and moving his left hand, as if he were feeling water. It seemed to Yasha that Volodya was pretending and waving his hand on purpose, and that he was watching him so as to grab Yasha the moment he touched him.

Feeling that he was going to choke the next instant, Yasha darted toward Volodya, seized his hand, blinked, hastily pulled Volodya's body upwards and was surprised that Volodya should follow him with such ease and so obediently. He came to the surface and breathed greedily—nothing was necessary or important to him now save being able to breathe and to feel his chest filling again and again with the wonderfully clean, sweet air.

Still holding Volodya's shirt, he began to push him toward the bank. He found it difficult to swim. When he could touch the bottom with his feet, Yasha laid Volodya on the bank, face downwards on the grass, and got out himself with difficulty. He shuddered on touching Volodya's cold body and seeing the dead, stony face. But he had to hurry even though he felt so tired and so wretched.

Turning Volodya over, he spread his arms, pressed on his diaphragm and blew into his nose. He was out of breath and felt weak, but Volodya still lay there, white and cold. "Dead?" Yasha thought in fright and felt terrified. If only he could run away and hide himself somewhere in order not to see that still, stony face!

Yasha sobbed with terror, jumped to his feet, grabbed Volodya by his feet, pulled upwards with all his might and, flushed with the effort, started shaking him. Volodya's head knocked against the ground and his hair became matted with mud. And when Yasha felt completely exhausted, had already lost heart and was ready to give up and run away, at that very instant water rushed out of Volodya's mouth, he groaned, and his body was seized by a convulsion. Yasha let Volodya's legs go, closed his eyes and sank down on the ground.

Volodya propped himself up on his weak arms, rose to his feet as if going to run away there and then, but collapsed, had another fit of convulsive coughing, spewing water and writhing in the wet grass.

Yasha crawled aside and, utterly exhausted, looked at Volodya. There was nobody now he loved more than Volodya and there was nothing in the world dearer to him than that pale, frightened and suffering face. A shy, loving smile shone in Yasha's eyes, he looked at Volodya with tenderness and kept asking foolishly:

"How is it, ah? How is it?"

Volodya recovered a little, wiped his face with his hand, looked at the water and said in a strange husky voice, noticeably straining himself and stammering: "How did I . . . ? I was drown-ing . . ."

Then Yasha all of a sudden wrinkled his face, blinked, tears rushed from his eyes and he burst out crying, weeping unconsolably, his whole body shaking. He was choking and ashamed of his tears. He was weeping for joy, for the terror he had gone through, for the thought that all had ended well and that Mishka Kayunenok had told a lie and there were no octopuses in that pool.

Volodya's eyes went dark, his mouth opened and he looked at Yasha in fright and puzzlement.

"What's the matter. . .with you?" he forced out.

"Yeah. . . ." Yasha uttered, trying his best not to cry and wiping his eyes with his trousers, "you do the drow . . . drowning . . . and me the sa . . . saving . . ."

And he sobbed even louder and with abandon.

Volodya blinked, twisted his face, looked again at the water, and his heart gave a shudder as he remembered everything.

"How . . . how I was drown-ing!" he said, as if in astonishment, and also burst out crying, jerking his thin shoulders, helplessly drooping his head and turning away from his saviour.

The water in the pool had long calmed down, the fish on Volodya's hook had got off, and the rod had been washed ashore. The sun was shining, the bushes, sprinkled with dew, were ablaze, and only the water in the pool remained dark.

The air had become warm and the horizon was dancing in its warm currents. Gusts of warm wind brought the scent of hay and sweet clover from faraway fields across the river. Blending with the more remote but still sharp smell of the wood, these scents and this warm breeze were like the breath of the earth that had awakened and was enjoying another bright day.

Translated by Lucy Nichols

Yuri Kazakov

Yuri Kazakov (1927–1982) was born in Moscow and graduated from the Gorky Literary Institute in 1958. His first work appeared in print in 1952. He authored many books of stories, including At a Small Station, A Wanderer, Two in December, A Northern Diary, You Bitterly Cried in Your Sleep, *and* Let Us Go to Lopshenga. *His books for children include* Tropics on the Stove, Arktur the Hound, *and* Teddy.

HOMESICK

Jean Fritz

IN MY FATHER'S study there was a large globe with all the countries of the world running around it. I could put my finger on the exact spot where I was and had been ever since I'd been born. And I was on the wrong side of the globe. I was in China in a city named Hankow, a dot on a crooked line that seemed to break the country right in two. The line was really the Yangtse River, but who would know by looking at a map what the Yangtse River really was?

Orange-brown, muddy mustard-colored. And wide, wide, wide. With a river smell that was old and came all the way up from the bottom. Sometimes old women knelt on the riverbank, begging the River God to return a son or grandson who may have drowned. They would wail and beat the earth to make the River God pay attention, but I knew how busy the River God must be. All those people on the Yangtse River! Coolies hauling water. Women washing clothes. Houseboats swarming with old people and young, chickens and pigs. Big crooked-sailed junks with eyes painted on their prows so they could see where they were going. I loved the Yangtse River, but, of course, I belonged on the other side of the world. In America with my grandmother.

Twenty-five fluffy little yellow chicks hatched from our eggs today, my grandmother wrote.

I wrote my grandmother that I had watched a Chinese magician swallow three yards of fire.

The trouble with living on the wrong side of the world was that I didn't feel like a *real* American.

For instance, I could never be president of the United States. I didn't want to be president; I wanted to be a writer. Still, why should there be a *law* saying that only a person born in the United States could be president? It was as if I wouldn't be American enough.

Actually, I was American every minute of the day, especially during school hours. I went to a British school and every morning we sang "God Save the King." Of course the British children loved singing about their gracious king. Ian Forbes stuck out his chest and sang as if he were saving the king all by himself. Everyone sang. Even Gina Boss who was Italian. And Vera Sebastian who was so Russian she dressed the way Russian girls did long ago before the Revolution when her family had to run away to keep from being killed.

But I wasn't Vera Sebastian. I asked my mother to write an excuse so I wouldn't have to sing, but she wouldn't do it. "When in Rome," she said, "do as the Romans do." What she meant was, "Don't make trouble. Just sing." So for a long time I did. I sang with my fingers crossed but still I felt like a traitor.

Then one day I thought: If my mother and father were really and truly in Rome, they wouldn't do what the Romans did at all. They'd probably try to get the Romans to do what *they* did, just as they were trying to teach the Chinese to do what Americans did. (My mother even gave classes in American manners.)

So that day I quit singing. I kept my mouth locked tight against the king of England. Our teacher, Miss Williams, didn't notice at first. She stood in front of the room, using a ruler for a baton, striking each syllable so hard it was as if she were making up for the times she had nothing to strike.

(Miss Williams was pinch-faced and bossy. Sometimes I wondered what had ever made her come to China. "Maybe to try and catch a husband," my mother said.

A husband! Miss Williams!)

"Make him vic-tor-i-ous," the class sang. It was on the strike of "vic" that Miss Williams noticed. Her eyes lighted on my mouth and when we sat down, she pointed her ruler at me.

"Is there something wrong with your voice today, Jean?" she asked.

"No, Miss Williams."

"You weren't singing."

"No, Miss Williams. It is not my national anthem."

"It is the national anthem we sing here," she snapped. "You have always sung. Even Vera sings it."

I looked at Vera with the big blue bow tied on the top of her head. Usually I felt sorry for her but not today. At recess I might even untie that bow, I thought. Just give it a yank. But if I'd been smart, I wouldn't have been looking at Vera. I would have been looking at Ian Forbes and I would have known that, no matter what Miss Williams said, I wasn't through with the king of England.

Recess at the British School was nothing I looked forward to. Every day we played a game called prisoner's base, which was all running and shouting and shoving and catching. I hated the game, yet everyone played except Vera Sebastian. She sat on the sidelines under her blue bow like someone who had been dropped out of a history book. By recess I had forgotten my plans for that bow. While everyone was getting ready for the game, I was as usual trying to look as if I didn't care if I was the last one picked for a team or not. I was leaning against the high stone wall that ran around the schoolyard. I was looking up at a little white cloud skittering across the sky when all at once someone tramped down hard on my right foot. Ian Forbes. Snarling bulldog face. Heel grinding down on my toes. Head thrust forward the way an animal might before it strikes.

"You wouldn't sing it. So say it," he ordered. "Let me hear you say it."

I tried to pull my foot away but he only ground down harder. "Say what?" I was telling my face please not to show what my foot felt.

"*God save the king*. Say it. Those four words. I want to hear you say it."

Although Ian Forbes was short, he was solid and tough and built for fighting. What was more, he always won. You had only to look at his bare knees between the top of his socks and his short pants to know that he would win. His knees were square. Bony and unbeatable. So of course it was crazy for me to argue with him.

"Why should I?" I asked. "Americans haven't said that since George the Third."

He grabbed my right arm and twisted it behind my back.

"Say it," he hissed.

I felt the tears come to my eyes and I hated myself for the tears. I hated myself for not staying in Rome the way my mother had told me.

"I'll never say it," I whispered.

They were choosing sides now in the schoolyard and Ian's name was being called–among the first as always.

He gave my arm another twist. "You'll sing tomorrow," he snarled, "or you'll be bloody sorry."

As he ran off, I slid to the ground, my head between my knees.

Oh, Grandma, I thought, why can't I be there with you? I'd feed the chickens for you. I'd pump water from the well, the way my father used to do.

It would be almost two years before we'd go to America. I was ten years old now; I'd be twelve then. But how could I think about *years?* I didn't even dare to think about the next day. After school I ran all the way home, fast so I couldn't think at all.

Our house stood behind a high stone wall which had chips of broken glass sticking up from the top to keep thieves away. I flung open the iron gate and threw myself through the front door.

"I'm home!" I yelled.

Then I remembered that it was Tuesday, the day my mother taught an English class at the Y.M.C.A. where my father was the director.

I stood in the hall, trying to catch my breath, and as always I began to feel small. It was a huge hall with ceilings so high it was as if they would have nothing to do with people. Certainly not with a mere child, not with me—the only child in the house. Once I asked my best friend, Andrea, if the hall made her feel little too. She said no. She was going to be a dancer and she loved space. She did a high kick to show how grand it was to have room.

Andrea Hull was a year older than I was and knew about everything sooner. She told me about commas, for instance, long before I took punctuation seriously. How could I write letters without commas? she asked. She made me so ashamed that for months I hung little wagging comma-tails all over the letters to my grandmother. She told me things that sounded so crazy I had to ask my mother if they were true. Like where babies came from. And that someday the whole world would end. My mother would frown when I asked her, but she always agreed that Andrea was right. It made me furious. How could she know such things and not tell me? What was the matter with grown-ups anyway?

I wished that Andrea were with me now, but she lived out in the country and I didn't see her often. Lin Nai-Nai, my amah, was the only one around, and of course I knew she'd be there. It was her job to stay with me when my parents were out. As soon as she heard me come in, she'd called, "Tsai loushang," which meant that she was upstairs. She might be mending or ironing but most likely she'd be sitting by the window embroidering. And she was. She even had my embroidery laid out, for we had made a bargain. She would teach me to embroider if I would teach her English. I liked embroidering: the cloth stretched tight within my embroidery hoop while I filled in the stamped pattern with cross-stitches and lazy daisy flowers. The trouble was that lazy daisies needed French knots for their centers and I hated making French knots. Mine always fell apart, so I left them to the end. Today I had twenty lazy daisies waiting for their knots.

Lin Nai-Nai had already threaded my needle with embroidery floss.

"Black centers," she said, "for the yellow flowers."

I felt myself glowering. "American flowers don't have centers," I said and gave her back the needle.

Lin Nai-Nai looked at me, puzzled, but she did not argue. She was different from other amahs. She did not even come from the servant class, although this was a secret we had to keep from the other servants who would have made her life miserable, had they known. She had run away from her husband when he had taken a second wife. She would always have been Wife Number One and the Boss no matter how many wives he had, but she would rather be no wife than head of a string of wives. She was modern. She might look old-fashioned, for her feet had been bound up tight when she was a little girl so that they would stay small, and now, like many Chinese women, she walked around on little stumps stuffed into tiny cloth shoes. Lin Nai-Nai's were embroidered with butterflies. Still, she believed in true love and one wife for one husband. We were good friends, Lin Nai-Nai and I, so I didn't know why I felt so mean.

She shrugged. "English lesson?" she asked, smiling.

I tested my arm to see if it still hurt from the twisting. It did. My foot too. "What do you want to know?" I asked.

We had been through the polite phrases—Please, Thank you, I beg your pardon, Excuse me, You're welcome, Merry Christmas (which she had practiced but hadn't had a chance to use since this was only October).

"If I meet an American on the street," she asked, "how do I greet him?"

I looked her straight in the eye and nodded my head in a greeting. "Sewing machine," I said. "You say, 'Sew-ing ma-chine.'"

She repeated after me, making the four syllables into four separate words. She got up and walked across the room, bowing and smiling. "Sew Ing Ma Shing."

Part of me wanted to laugh at the thought of Lin Nai-Nai maybe meeting Dr. Carhart, our minister, whose face would surely puff up, the way it always did when he was flustered. But part of me didn't want to laugh at all. I didn't like it when my feelings got tangled, so I ran downstairs and played chopsticks on the piano. Loud and fast. When my sore arm hurt, I just beat on the keys harder.

Then I went out to the kitchen to see if Yang Sze-Fu, the cook, would give me something to eat. I found him reading a Chinese newspaper, his eyes going up and down with the characters. (Chinese words don't march across flat surfaces the way ours do; they drop down cliffs, one cliff after another from right to left across a page.)

"Can I have a piece of cinnamon toast?" I asked. "And a cup of cocoa?"

Yang Sze-Fu grunted. He was smoking a cigarette, which he wasn't supposed to do in the kitchen, but Yang Sze-Fu mostly did what he wanted. He considered himself superior to common workers. You could tell because of the fingernails on his pinkies. They were at least two inches long, which was his way of showing that he didn't have to use his hands for rough or dirty work. He didn't seem to care that his fingernails were dirty, but maybe he couldn't keep such long nails clean.

He made my toast while his cigarette dangled out of the corner of his mouth, collecting a long ash that finally fell on the floor. He wouldn't have kept smoking if my mother had been there, although he didn't always pay attention to my mother. Never about butter pagodas, for instance. No matter how many times my mother told him before a dinner party, "No butter pagoda," it made no difference. As soon as everyone was seated, the serving boy, Wong Sze-Fu, would bring in a pagoda and set it on the table. The guests would "oh" and "ah," for it was a masterpiece: a pagoda molded out of butter, curved roofs rising tier upon tier, but my mother could only think how unsanitary it was. For, of course, Yang Sze-Fu had molded the butter with his hands and carved the decorations with one of his long fingernails. Still, we always used the butter, for if my mother sent it back to the kitchen, Yang Sze-Fu would lose face and quit.

When my toast and cocoa were ready, I took them upstairs to my room (the blue room) and while I ate, I began *Sara Crewe* again. Now there was a girl, I thought, who was worth crying over. I wasn't going to think about myself. Or Ian Forbes. Or the next day. I wasn't. I wasn't.

And I didn't. Not all afternoon. Not all evening. Still, I must have decided what I was going to do because the next morning when I started for school and came to the corner where the man sold hot chestnuts, the corner where I always turned to go to school, I didn't turn. I walked straight ahead. I wasn't going to school that day.

I walked toward the Yangtse River. Past the store that sold paper pellets that opened up into flowers when you dropped them in a glass of water. Then up the block where the beggars sat. I never saw anyone give money to a beggar. You couldn't, my father explained, or you'd be mobbed by beggars. They'd follow you everyplace;

they'd never leave you alone. I had learned not to look at them when I passed and yet I saw. The running sores, the twisted legs, the mangled faces. What I couldn't get over was that, like me, each one of those beggars had only one life to live. It just happened that they had drawn rotten ones.

Oh, Grandma, I thought, we may be far apart but we're lucky, you and I. Do you even know how lucky? In America do you know?

This part of the city didn't actually belong to the Chinese, even though the beggars sat there, even though upper-class Chinese lived there. A long time ago other countries had just walked into China and divided up part of Hankow (and other cities) into sections, or concessions, which they called their own and used their own rules for governing. We lived in the French concession on Rue de Paris. Then there was the British concession and the Japanese. The Russian and German concessions had been officially returned to China, but the people still called them concessions. The Americans didn't have one, although, like some of the other countries, they had gunboats on the river. In case, my father said. In case what? Just in case. That's all he'd say.

The concessions didn't look like the rest of China. The buildings were solemn and orderly with little plots of grass around them. Not like those in the Chinese part of the city: a jumble of rickety shops with people, vegetables, crates of quacking ducks, yard goods, bamboo baskets, and mangy dogs spilling onto a street so narrow it was hardly there.

The grandest street in Hankow was the Bund, which ran along beside the Yangtse River. When I came to it after passing the beggars, I looked to my left and saw the American flag flying over the American consulate building. I was proud of the flag and I thought maybe today it was proud of me. It flapped in the breeze as if it were saying ha-ha to the king of England.

Then I looked to the right at the Customs House, which stood at the other end of the Bund. The clock on top of the tower said nine-thirty. How would I spend the day?

I crossed the street to the promenade part of the Bund. When people walked here, they weren't usually going anyplace; they were just out for the air. My mother would wear her broad-brimmed beaver hat when we came and my father would swing his cane in that jaunty way that showed how glad he was to be a man. I thought I would just sit on a bench for the morning. I would watch the Customs House clock, and when it was time, I would eat the lunch I had brought along in my schoolbag.

I was the only one sitting on a bench. People did not generally "take the air" on a Wednesday morning and besides, not everyone was allowed here. The British had put a sign on the Bund, NO DOGS, NO CHINESE. This meant that I could never bring Lin Nai-Nai with me. My father couldn't even bring his best friend, Mr. T. K. Hu. Maybe the British wanted a place where they could pretend they weren't in China, I thought. Still, there were always Chinese coolies around. In order to load and unload boats in the river, coolies had to cross the Bund. All day they went back and forth, bent double under their loads, sweating and chanting in a tired, singsong way that seemed to get them from one step to the next.

To pass the time, I decided to recite poetry. The one good thing about Miss Williams was that she made us learn poems by heart and I liked that. There was one particular poem I didn't want to forget. I looked at the Yangtse River and pretended that all the busy people in the boats were my audience.

" 'Breathes there the man, with soul so dead,' " I cried, " 'Who never to himself hath said, This is my own, my native land!' "

I was so carried away by my performance that I didn't notice the policeman until he was right in front of me. Like all policemen in the British concession, he was a bushy-bearded Indian with a red turban wrapped around his head.

He pointed to my schoolbag. "Little miss," he said, "why aren't you in school?"

He was tall and mysterious-looking, more like a character in my Arabian Nights book than a man you expected to talk to. I fumbled for an answer. "I'm going on an errand," I said finally. "I just sat down for a rest." I picked up my schoolbag and walked quickly away. When I looked around, he was back on his corner, directing traffic.

So now they were chasing children away too, I thought angrily. Well, I'd like to show them. Someday I'd like to walk a dog down the whole length of the Bund. A Great Dane. I'd have him on a leash–like this–(I put out my hand as if I were holding a leash right then) and he'd be so big and strong I'd have to strain to hold him back (I strained). Then of course sometimes he'd have to do his business and I'd stop (like this) right in the middle of the sidewalk and let him go to it. I was so busy with my Great Dane I was at the end of the Bund before I knew it. I let go of the leash, clapped my hands, and told my dog to go home. Then I left the Bund and the concessions and walked into the Chinese world.

My mother and father and I had walked here but not for many months. This part near the river was called the Mud Flats. Sometimes it was muddier than others, and when the river flooded, the flats disappeared underwater. Sometimes even the fishermen's huts were washed away, knocked right off their long-legged stilts and swept down the river. But today the river was fairly low and the mud had dried so that it was cracked and cakey. Most of the men who lived here were out fishing, some not far from the shore, poling their sampans through the shallow water. Only a few people were on the flats: a man cleaning fish on a flat rock at the water's edge, a woman spreading clothes on the dirt to dry, a few small children. But behind the huts was something I had never seen before. Even before I came close, I guessed what it was. Even then, I was excited by the strangeness of it.

It was the beginnings of a boat. The skeleton of a large junk, its ribs lying bare, its backbone running straight and true down the bottom. The outline of the prow was already in place, turning up wide and snub-nosed, the way all junks did. I had never thought of boats starting from nothing, of taking on bones under their bodies. The eyes, I supposed, would be the last thing added. Then the junk would have life.

The builders were not there and I was behind the huts where no one could see me as I walked around and around, marveling. Then I climbed inside and as I did, I knew that something wonderful was happening to me. I was a-tingle, the way a magician must feel when he swallows fire, because suddenly I knew that the boat was mine. No matter who really owned it, it was mine. Even if I never saw it again, it would be my junk sailing up and down the Yangtse River. My junk seeing the river sights with its two eyes, seeing them for me whether I was there or not. Often I had tried to put the Yangtse River into a poem so I could keep it. Sometimes I had tried to draw it, but nothing I did ever came close. But now, *now* I had my junk and somehow that gave me the river too.

I thought I should put my mark on the boat. Perhaps on the side of the spine. Very small. A secret between the boat and me. I opened my schoolbag and took out my folding penknife that I used for sharpening pencils. Very carefully I carved the Chinese character that was our name. Gau. (In China my father was Mr. Gau, my mother was Mrs. Gau, and I was Little Miss Gau.) The builders would paint right over the character, I thought, and never notice. But I would know. Always and forever I would know.

For a long time I dreamed about the boat, imagining it finished, its sails up, its eyes wide. Someday it might sail all the way down the Yangtse to Shanghai, so I told the boat what it would see along the way because I had been there and the boat hadn't. After a while I got hungry and I ate my egg sandwich. I was in the midst of peeling an orange when all at once I had company.

A small boy, not more than four years old, wandered around to the back of the huts, saw me, and stopped still. He was wearing a ragged blue cotton jacket with a red cloth, pincushion-like charm around his neck which was supposed to keep him from getting smallpox. Sticking up straight from the middle of his head was a small pigtail which I knew was to fool the gods and make them think he was a girl. (Gods didn't bother much with girls; it was boys that were important in China.) The weather was still warm so he wore no pants, nothing below the waist. Most small boys went around like this so that when they had to go, they could just let loose and go. He walked slowly up to the boat, stared at me, and then nodded as if he'd already guessed what I was. "Foreign devil," he announced gravely.

I shook my head. "No," I said in Chinese. "American friend." Through the ribs of the boat, I handed him a segment of orange. He ate it slowly, his eyes on the rest of the orange. Segment by segment, I gave it all to him. Then he wiped his hands down the front of his jacket.

"Foreign devil," he repeated.

"American friend," I corrected. Then I asked him about the boat. Who was building it? Where were the builders?

He pointed with his chin upriver. "Not here today. Back tomorrow."

I knew it would only be a question of time before the boy would run off to alert the people in the huts. "Foreign devil, foreign devil," he would cry. So I put my hand on the prow of the boat, wished it luck, and climbing out, I started back toward the Bund. To my surprise the boy walked beside me. When we came to the edge of the Bund, I squatted down so we would be on the same eye level. "Good-bye," I said. "May the River God protect you."

For a moment the boy stared. When he spoke, it was as if he were trying out a new sound. "American friend," he said slowly.

When I looked back, he was still there, looking soberly toward the foreign world to which I had gone.

The time, according to the Customs House clock, was five after two, which meant that I couldn't go home for two hours. School was dismissed at three-thirty and I was home by three-forty-five unless I had to stay in for talking in class. It took me about fifteen minutes to write "I will not talk in class" fifty times, and so I often came home at four o'clock. (I wrote up and down like the Chinese: fifty "I's," fifty "wills," and right through the sentence so I never had to think what I was writing. It wasn't as if I were making a promise.) Today I planned to arrive home at four, my "staying-in" time, in the hope that I wouldn't meet classmates on the way.

Meanwhile I wandered up and down the streets, in and out of stores. I weighed myself on the big scale in the Hankow Dispensary and found that I was as skinny as ever. I went to the Terminus Hotel and tried out the chairs in the lounge. At first I didn't mind wandering about like this. Half of my mind was still on the river with my junk, but as time went on, my junk began slipping away until I was alone with nothing but questions. Would my mother find out about today? How could I skip school tomorrow? And the next day and the next? Could I get sick? Was there a kind of long lie-abed sickness that didn't hurt?

I arrived home at four, just as I had planned, opened the door, and called out, "I'm home!" Cheery-like and normal. But I was scarcely in the house before Lin Nai-Nai ran to me from one side of the hall and my mother from the other.

"Are you all right? Are you all right?" Lin Nai-Nai felt my arms as if she expected them to be broken. My mother's face was white. "What happened?" she asked.

Then I looked through the open door into the living room and saw Miss Williams sitting there. She had beaten me home and asked about my absence, which of course had scared everyone. But now my mother could see that I was in one piece and for some reason this seemed to make her mad. She took me by the hand and led me into the living room. "Miss Williams said you weren't in school," she said. "Why was that?"

I hung my head, just the way cowards do in books.

My mother dropped my hand. "Jean will be in school tomorrow," she said firmly. She walked Miss Williams to the door. "Thank you for stopping by."

Miss Williams looked satisfied in her mean, pinched way. "Well," she said, "ta-ta." (She always said "ta-ta" instead of "good-bye." Chicken language, it sounded like.)

As soon as Miss Williams was gone and my mother was sitting down again, I burst into tears. Kneeling on the floor, I buried my head in her lap and poured out the whole miserable story. My mother could see that I really wasn't in one piece after all, so she listened quietly, stroking my hair as I talked, but gradually I could feel her stiffen. I knew she was remembering that she was a mother.

"You better go up to your room," she said, "and think things over. We'll talk about it after supper."

I flung myself on my bed. What was there to think? Either I went to school and got beaten up. Or I quit.

After supper I explained to my mother and father how simple it was. I could stay at home and my mother could teach me, the way Andrea's mother taught her. Maybe I could even go to Andrea's house and study with her.

My mother shook her head. Yes, it was simple, she agreed. I could go back to the British School, be sensible, and start singing about the king again.

I clutched the edge of the table. Couldn't she understand? I couldn't turn back now. It was too late.

So far my father had not said a word. He was leaning back, teetering on the two hind legs of his chair, the way he always did after a meal, the way that drove my mother crazy. But he was not the kind of person to keep all four legs of a chair on the floor just because someone wanted him to. He wasn't a turning-back person so I hoped maybe he would understand. As I watched him, I saw a twinkle start in his eyes and suddenly he brought his chair down slam-bang flat on the floor. He got up and motioned for us to follow him into the living room. He sat down at the piano and began to pick out the tune for "God Save the King."

A big help, I thought. Was he going to make me practice?

Then he began to sing:

"My country 'tis of thee,

Sweet land of liberty, . . ."

Of course! It was the same tune. Why hadn't I thought of that? Who would know what I was singing as long as I moved my lips? I joined in now, loud and strong.

"Of thee I sing."

My mother laughed in spite of herself. "If you sing that loud," she said, "you'll start a revolution."

"Tomorrow I'll sing softly," I promised. "No one will know." But for now I really let freedom ring.

Then all at once I wanted to see Lin Nai-Nai. I ran out back, through the courtyard that separated the house from the servants' quarters, and upstairs to her room.

"It's me," I called through the door and when she opened up, I threw my arms around her. "Oh, Lin Nai-Nai, I love you," I said. "You haven't said it yet, have you?"

"Said what?"

"Sewing machine. You haven't said it?"

"No," she said, "not yet. I'm still practicing."

"Don't say it, Lin Nai-Nai. Say 'Good day.' It's shorter and easier. Besides, it's more polite."

"Good day?" she repeated.

"Yes, that's right. Good day." I hugged her and ran back to the house.

The next day at school when we rose to sing the British national anthem, everyone stared at me, but as soon as I opened my mouth, the class lost interest. All but Ian Forbes. His eyes never left my face, but I sang softly, carefully, proudly. At recess he sauntered over to where I stood against the wall.

He spat on the ground. "You can be bloody glad you sang today," he said. Then he strutted off as if he and those square knees of his had won again.

And, of course, I was bloody glad.

Jean Fritz

Jean Fritz was born in Hankow, China, in 1915. She graduated from Wheaton College in Norton, Massachusetts, and studied at Columbia University. She is generally acknowledged as being one of the best authors of historical biographies written for young people. Her well-crafted, realistic, thoroughly researched, and frequently witty books look at the characters that have shaped American history. She has written about Ben Franklin, Christopher Columbus, John Hancock, Paul Revere, Sam Adams, and many other prominent historical figures. Among her numerous awards are the Boston Globe-Horn Honor Book Award, the American Book Award, and the Newbery Honor Book Award, all of which were given for her book Homesick: My Own Story. *Many of her books have been honored by the American Library Association.*

THE TUBETEIKA AFFAIR

Vytaute Zilinskaite

DOTAS CHARGED only a trifle for his advice: one stamp. It could even be a used stamp. Money? Oh no, he wanted none of that. There had been a time when he had charged five kopecks, but his parents had heard about it. So from then on he took only stamps.

The fame of the wise counsellor Dotas in 3B had long ago spread through the school; but after the tubeteika affair was settled, thanks to his ingenuity, it spread far beyond its walls.

But let us go back to the beginning.

Spring had come with a rush. The thin white curtains could not withstand the sun and it poured in through the large windows onto the children. Now, who could be dull or depressed on such a day? There was not a single sombre face, the mood was one of spring gaiety—except for Andrius. He was obviously worried. During break he had hovered around the class wiseacre, evidently with a problem. But Dotas took no notice, played hard to get. So it was only after school was out and they were on their way home that he overtook Dotas in the street and their historic consultation took place.

"Dotas! Wait for me!" Andrius called. "If you can't help me I'm done for!"

The trouble was this. Andrius's father had recently returned from Kirghizia—so far off, that if you went there by train it would take four whole days! But Andrius's father had flown. It was quite different from Lithuania there, he said, all mountains, one after the other, like caravans of camels with grey humps, and snow on top of them. And between the mountains there were valleys with green grass and bright red poppies. But that was not the main thing. Dad had brought back a kind of cap–black, with four corners and embroidered in white silk. It was called a tubeteika–you pronounced it "tyubbytaker." Dad showed it around and then put it in a cupboard, alongside a sombrero–a broad straw hat from Argentina, and a svanka–a white felt cap from the Caucasus. "The start of our family collection of national headdresses," said Dad.

Yesterday, Sunday, Andrius had taken the cap without permission. He wanted to show it off–although actually it was too big for him and kept slipping down over his nose instead of sitting smartly on the back of his head. Well, to make a long story short, he set off in the tubeteika to the bank of the Vilnia. And bent over the water–and the tubeteika slid forward and–

"I ran along the bank and tried to keep up with it. I simply tore along but by the bridge–you know?–the water swirls around, a real whirlpool–and it was gone. Sucked down."

"And they don't know yet at home," said Dotas, half statement, half question.

"Would I be picking your brains if they knew?" sobbed Andrius, then, remembering, felt in his pocket and pulled out a stamp with a zebra and a chocolate in silver paper. The stamp was crumpled and the sweet had been flattened from long existence in his pocket. He held out his gifts to Dotas.

Dotas examined the stamp and then returned it.

"Defective—a reject."

"I didn't know," mumbled a confused Andrius. "I'll get you another. A whole series, with spiders!"

Dotas nodded staidly and relapsed into concentrated thought, chewing the chocolate. Promising folds appeared on his forehead.

"Listen, then. Ask your father what is the capital of Kirghizia. Secondly, how many schools there are. Only do it so that he doesn't suspect anything. That's all," he said at last.

"That's all?" repeated Andrius, disappointed.

"For the present–all. The rest comes later," said Dotas with a sly look. "Find out, and tell me." He turned on his heel and ran off home.

Just before going to bed that evening Andrius tackled his father, approaching in roundabout ways.

"Dad, what's the capital of Portugal?"

"Lisbon."

"Lisbon? And Estonia?"

"You ought to know that! Tallinn."

"Oh, of course–I'd forgotten. And Kirghizia?"

"Kirghizia? Frunze."

"Frunze, Frunze, Frunze," he whispered to fix it in his mind. "And Dad! How many schools would there be in Frunze?"

"A good many, for certain."

"As many as thirty?"

"I expect so. They have a lot of children there."

"Thirty schools. And the forms–I suppose they have them like ours–three A, three B, and so on all through the school."

"Of course. A and B and maybe C, D and E. I told you there are a lot of children."

"Smashing!"

"I'm glad to see you taking an interest in distant parts," said Dad approvingly. "You can always ask me if there's anything you want to know, I'll be glad to tell you."

"Not less than thirty," Dotas repeated thoughtfully after he had heard Andrius's report during the first break. He did not hurry with his advice, and indeed, it seemed doubtful whether he had any to give because he suddenly asked, "What's your number in the form book?"

"Fifteen."

"Fifteen—that's better, in fact it's good," he mumbled. "Now, this is what you must do. Write to Frunze. To a pupil who is number fifteen in form 3B."

"But what shall I write?"

"Send some kind of souvenir–a postcard or a badge or something, and ask for a tubeteika."

"So that's it!"

So clever and yet so simple! Couldn't be simpler. Why couldn't he have thought of that himself? Obviously he felt disgusted with himself.

Dotas looked at him, narrow-eyed, and he suddenly wondered uneasily whether the wiseacre could read his thoughts and perhaps take offense.

"What a grand idea!" he flattered his counselor.

"Don't write only one letter," said the latter weightily. "Nothing might come of it. Write to all the thirty schools, address the letters school number one, two and so on, Frunze, Kirghizia. Pupil number fifteen in form three B–the three A and C too, all the threes."

"How many letters will that be? Surely I don't need so many."

"Better be safe. Let's see–four forms each in thirty schools–h'm! A hundred and twenty. Well, that makes it a sure thing, one of the hundred and twenty will certainly send it."

"Well—thanks awfully!"

"That's all right. If they send two, then one for me?"

"Of course!"

Then the work began. Andrius cut the pages of ten notebooks into neat sheets, emptied his collection of badges and pulled all the unused stamps out of his album. A hundred and twenty letters–that was no joke, he had not written so many in his whole life.

> Dear unknown friend,
>
> I do not yet know your name, but like me you are number fifteen in the form book and for that reason I am writing to you. I have had a piece of very bad luck. My dad was in Kirghizia and brought back a souvenir. A black tubeteika with white embroidery. And I accidentally dropped it in the river. Dad does not know yet but when he does there'll be bad trouble. Please save me, send me a tubeteika, and then let's go on corresponding. I am enclosing a souvenir, a badge from my city Vilnius. Write to me at school so that they do not know at home. That's all. All the best,
>
> Andrius

"That's all right," said Dotas when Andrius showed him the letter and then asked him to add, "Dotas, a representative of Lithuanian youth, sends you greetings and would be very glad to make your acquaintance."

Andrius sighed but wrote it. A hundred and twenty times.

A week passed and then a second. Dad went away on another trip without discovering the loss of the tubeteika. Andrius lived in a torment of suspense until at last, one day in May, the teacher suddenly said, "Andrius, there's a parcel for you in the teacher's room, go and fetch it."

Andrius went with beating heart. A package wrapped in pink paper lay on the long table. Andrius picked it up, went out into the passage, then with trembling hands tore off the paper and pulled out–a tubeteika!–exactly like the one Dad had brought, black, four-cornered and embroidered with white silk. Marvelous! And there was a letter, too.

Dear Andrius,

I was very pleased to get your letter. Thank you for the badge. I bought a tubeteika at once and am glad to give it to you. I have wanted for a long time to have a pen-friend in another republic. My mother says that there are no mountains in Lithuania and that you do not drink koumiss, that is mare's milk. A pity because koumiss is very good, I love it. I collect butterflies, I have a lot. If you can, please catch a Lithuanian butterfly for me. Write me more about yourself and your friends and your school and your republic. And I will write, too. Greetings to your youth representative Dotas,

All the best,

Asan

Returning to the classroom, Andrius met Dotas's eyes. He wore a proudly triumphant look. They exchanged winks.

The next day again the teacher announced a parcel for Andrius.

Again Andrius stood before the long table—but this time he saw four packages. He did not even wait to open them—the contents were obvious; he scooped them up and scuttled back to the classroom. One tubeteika he would give the wiseacre as agreed, one for himself, but the third and fourth and fifth—? Oh, something would turn up.

After school Dotas tried on the tubeteika in the cloakroom.

"A bit big, but it'll do."

You might at least have said thank you, thought Andrius.

When the teacher summoned Andrius the next day she sounded puzzled.

Andrius went reluctantly, very unhappy, his legs like rubber. And with reason. The whole table was piled with almost identical packages. A mountain of them! Fifty at least, maybe more. How on earth would he carry them all? And what was he to do with them?

In his confusion it took him a long time to gather them up. And it was all the fault of that clever donkey Dotas.

Andrius carried the packages to the cloakroom, rolled them in his raincoat and tied the sleeves. When he returned to the classroom he did not even look at Dotas; but after school he grabbed the bundle and ran to overtake him, to give them all to him and let him do what he liked with them since he was so clever. However, Dotas heard panting behind him, turned, saw Andrius crimson with fury, and ran for his life.

"Stop!" howled Andrius. "Stop! These are yours! You hear me? Yours! You told me to write all those letters! Take them or I'll tell the teacher!"

But Dotas pelted off without turning.

When he got home Andrius dived into the cellar, found a clean sack, tipped all the packages into it, pushed it into a corner and covered it with all sorts of old rubbish. Later, he could get it out, read the letters and seek advice from his own wits, how on earth to get out of this new snarl he was in.

At school he kept very quiet. He did not want to be noticed. He never looked at Dotas.

At break the headmaster himself sought him out.

"I think you'd better explain the meaning of all this. Otherwise I'll have to send for your parents."

The pile of packages on the table in the teachers' room was as big as ever. Andrius looked at it, horrified.

"I–I'll explain–later," he whispered and rather surprisingly the headmaster left it at that.

It certainly was a case of out of the frying-pan. Andrius again collected the armful of packages, took them to the cloakroom and bundled them into his coat. Dotas had prudently disappeared without waiting for the last lesson.

The sack in the cellar was almost full and nearly too heavy to lift.

Later on he discovered a package he had pushed into his pocket and forgotten. He unwrapped it and saw a tubeteika–*such* a tubeteika, velvet, and embroidered with blue silk, and it fitted him perfectly, too. And a letter.

> Dear distant Andrius,
>
> What an unusual name but a nice one. The whole form envied me being the fifteenth and getting a letter from Lithuania. I was dreadfully upset about your needing a tubeteika so badly because I have not any money to buy one and send it at once. And I cannot ask mum. Dad was killed in a motor accident and I have nine brothers and sisters, three older than I am and the rest younger, so it is difficult for mum with all of us. But I asked auntie for velvet and silk and my sisters and friends have helped me. They all send you greetings. Do you like our tubeteika? I am so glad to give it to you, Andrius. My grandad and grandma live on the bank of a great big lake called Issyk-Kul. It is beautiful there. Come and see it when you grow up. I must stop now but I shall be waiting for your reply. I would like to have you for a pen-friend.
>
> Wishing you all the very best,
>
> Aigyul

Reading the letter Andrius felt himself blush for shame. He remembered it in the night and cried. He cried for a long time, and in the morning his whole face was swollen.

That day there were only three packages on the table. The flood was dwindling. The day after there was only a letter.

> "Dear Andrius," wrote a boy called Tologen, "I am sorry I cannot send you a tubeteika, I feel very bad about it but it is not my fault. I have been to all the shops where they have

always had tubeteikas but now there was not one, they told me they had had plenty but they were all sold out. Actually, it is girls who wear tubeteikas here, boys wear a kind of felt hat with two little peaks. It is called ak-kalpak and it is boat-shaped. But please do not worry, as soon as any appear I will send you a tubeteika. I would like to have you for a pen-friend. I am enclosing a picture postcard of the Ala-Tau Mountains. And please do send me pictures of Lithuania, especially the sea. I have never seen the sea but on the map Lithuania is right by it. Honestly, I tried to get you the tubeteika."

Andrius read this letter in the classroom during break and he had hardly finished when the monitor came and said the headmaster wanted him and added that the form mistress was already in his office.

To say Andrius was uncomfortable would be putting it mildly. He stared at his boots and his ears burned. And then–suddenly–he decided to make a clean breast of it all.

"But why did you send a hundred and twenty letters?" asked the headmaster. "Wouldn't one have been enough?"

"It was Dotas who advised me to." Andrius was no tell-tale, but since Dotas was avoiding him, then let people know the sort of adviser he was. "I wanted to write one but he said it must be a hundred and twenty. It took me three days, my hands were sore, and then he made me add a greeting from him."

Now Dotas will get it, thought Andrius vengefully. Serve him right!

But the teacher only laughed. "You don't have to follow every bit of advice that's given. Use your own head! You're a head taller than he is and you get better marks, too!"

His eyes went down to his boots again. He was crimson with

shame. It was true, he ought to have done his own thinking. He wasn't a bit of a kid. He would soon be in the fourth form.

At the end of the last lesson the teacher gave Dotas a meaning look.

"Well, wise adviser, what has your wisdom to offer now? You know what I'm talking about?"

"I know," said Dotas without any great sign of confusion.

"And what's your advice now?"

Dotas stared out of the window. It gave a view of the railway and a train with small green coaches, looking like toys in the distance. A fold appeared on the forehead of the sage.

Everybody knew the whole story by this time and all eyes were fixed on Dotas. How would he wriggle out of this one?

"My advice is," said Dotas with dignity, "to distribute the tubeteikas and letters to all those who'd like to have pen-friends in Kirghizia. There!"

"Good for you!" said the teacher.

The form literally howled with delight and Andrius felt as though he had been sandbagged. Idiot–such a simple solution! Couldn't be simpler! Hand around the tubeteikas and let the kids answer the letters and have pen-friends and exchange souvenirs. Why hadn't he thought of it himself? Of course, he might have, but Dotas had thought of it first. It wasn't for nothing the kids said he'd a head on him!

It wasn't worth bearing a grudge against Dotas. There was too much to be done. He dragged the sack into the classroom and it wasn't only his pals from 3B who wanted to correspond with children in Kirghizia. A and C too were clamoring for letters. Andrius kept Asan and Aigyul for himself, however. They would be his own friends.

Now the whole form dreams of visiting the Ala-Tau Mountains and Lake Issyk-Kul. They probably will, too, if not this summer, then the next. Dotas advises it, too.

Translated by Eve Manning

Vytaute Zilinskaite

Vytaute Zilinskaite is a Lithuanian writer, born in 1930 in Kaunas. In 1955 she graduated from Vilnius University. Her works, the first published in 1958, include collections of poetry, satirical stories,and a short novel entitled My Hatred Is Stronger. *Her books for children include* The Robot and the Butterfly *and* Mike the Giant. *She is twice winner of the State Prize of Lithuania and lives in Vilnius.*

THE JOKE

Radii Pogodin

IT SEEMED DONYKA'S parents had brought him to the ends of the earth to live in the small town. You see, young Donyka didn't have any grandmother who smelled of pies or pancakes or strawberry jam, no grandfather who read the morning newspaper in the kitchen before everyone else was awake. Donyka had only his mother and his father, and his mother and father only had him, so there had been no one else to leave him with. And his parents, who were scientists, had never planned to live in the town; shortly after arriving, the two of them had gone out over the arctic snow on a winter expedition to do research. And so Donyka had to stay and live at the school. It was a boarding school—all the children lived there.

But then eight-year-old Donyka was used to boarding schools. When he was of nursery school age, he had lived at the nursery school. When he was of kindergarten age, he lived at the kindergarten school. Only on Saturdays and Sundays did he get to see his parents those years. But at the new school he would see them even less, perhaps only four times during the whole long winter.

The town on the northern sea was tiny, but busy and well known as an arctic port. In the winter, snowed-in ships stayed in the harbor waiting for summer. In the summer, the waters teemed with ships. As winter came on again, convoys of cargo ships heavy with all kinds of interesting freight were constantly departing, waiting their turn to go through the pathways left in the ice, then scurrying to reach the open sea. That's the kind of town it was.

At the school Donyka lived with two other boys in one room. One boy, Lyonka, was the son of a professional trapper, while the other, Sanyka, was the son of a radio operator. Born the same year, the boys were almost the same age. As a rule, the parents of all three received frequent commendations about the boys by radio. But something happened one winter day about which none of their parents was ever told.

No, there were no radio reports to the parents that day.

It happened on a Sunday. Sanyka, whose little brother, Stas, was a boarder in the school's nursery, had brought him to their room to visit. But the boys played with Stas for some time and Sanyka was getting ready to take Stas back across the yard to his own dormitory when they heard an announcement of a "weather watch" over the radio: a blizzard was expected. In a blizzard, the wind blowing across the arctic town is unbelievably fierce. Pilots have to strap their planes down to specially constructed poles. Townspeople are afraid to leave their homes—the wind can knock them down or throw them against a rock, in which case they would immediately be covered with the swirling snow, and there you'd have it, a tragedy.

Young and old, everyone in the port town knew to fear a blizzard. But, on that day, third-grader Lyonka, something of a know-it-all among the three, knew better.

"Donyka, Sanyka," he said, after hearing the warning, "let's go to the island. They're showing a good movie today." It was nearly two miles across the frozen, barren sound to the island where the movie was being shown.

"How can we?" Donyka said. "There's a blizzard coming!"

"We'll make it over there before the blizzard comes if we run fast," Lyonka said.

"Not me. I can't," Sanyka told him. "I have Stas. Look at him, he's fat, his clothes are bulky. He couldn't run fast if he wanted to."

"I can run faster than all of you," Stas said, "only I don't want to." He yawned. "I want to take a nap."

That only encouraged Lyonka. "Good boy, Stas, take a nap. Why don't you go on over to the dormitory now. We'll just run over to the island and be back before you know it."

At that very moment the radio crackled another warning: the blizzard was very close, townspeople were not to leave their homes. Those who happened to be outside were advised to find shelter wherever they could to protect themselves from the wind.

Sanyka was annoyed. "Now we're even too late to get Stas back! You'll have to stay here with us now, Stas."

But that was when Lyonka had his great idea. "I've got it!" he said. "Let's write a note saying that the four of us have gone over to the island to see the movie. Let's put on our coats, but get under our beds and hide. Everyone will get worried, but we'll be right here. It'll be a joke!"

Donyka looked at Lyonka for a moment. "Let's do it," he said, and finally Sanyka agreed. It was just a joke.

Quickly, the three friends tore a page out of a lined notebook and wrote their note. Then they dressed as if they were going outside, bundling little Stas up too, and crawled under their beds. The trouble was that in the warmth and darkness under the beds, before long all four boys fell asleep.

The blizzard warnings were still crackling across the airwaves when a counselor happened to pass by the boys' room. Glancing in, she did not see anyone there, but she saw the note on the table and read it. She ran straight to the director's office. The director read the note and went straight to the telephone.

Terribly upset, he walked around and around his desk as he

spoke: "We have a problem here. Four of the boys from our school have gone out to the island!"

"What!" answered the man at the other end, a town official. "What are the boys' names?"

"Lonyka, Sanyka, and Donyka . . . and they have a preschooler with them. His name is Stas."

"I understand," the man said. "We won't inform the parents yet, no use worrying them. I'll take all necessary measures here." The man put the phone down but immediately picked it up again and called the harbormaster.

"We have an alert. Get your sailors out. Some boys have gone to the island. Yes, in the storm. You'll need searchlights and rope. . . ."

He called the chief of the hydraulic engineers corps. "We have an alert! Three boys and a preschooler are out on the sound in the blizzard! Get your all-terrain vehicles out there. Move toward the ocean, yes, toward the blizzard."

He telephoned the island and spoke to the air commander and the chief of meteorology. "We have an alert! Four youngsters out on the sound in the blizzard. Get your people out. Start walking toward the port; we'll be walking from this direction."

He called the superintendent at the check-point headquarters for hunters and trappers. "We have an alert! Four boys are stuck out on the sound in the blizzard. Do you have any dogs and sleds available?"

"Yes, we do," came the answer at the other end. "A couple of trappers are here waiting out the storm."

"Good, let them get the sleds out. They should move in front of the all-terrain vehicles, move toward the ocean." And then he called the military commander. In minutes the soldiers were out, forming a human chain and moving out into the blizzard. As they pushed their way into the wind, they looked behind every ice mound and into every crevice.

Then the man gathered all the other townspeople and, together with them, went out into the blizzard.

The blizzard was going full force by now, the wind beating against any rock or obstacle in its way, whizzing through any path, blowing and howling so much, that it sounded like one long explosion. Out on the frozen ice the blizzard whistled and whined fiercely, flowing across the sound as if it were a layer of lava sweeping away the snowy surface. At times the crackling and howling were almost like laughter.

Meanwhile, the three older boys were fast asleep under their beds, their bodies all steamy and warm, wrapped up in their big coats. Little Stas lay next to them asleep, too, snoring and mumbling something as he dreamed some sweet dream.

On the ice, people were tied to each other with ropes, the blizzard blowing them down as they struggled to find their way. The light from their flashlights shone no farther than a step ahead of them. The all-terrain vehicles rumbled along, their sounds lost in the blizzard's wind, their strong headlights shining only a few paces in front of the big machines. Dogsleds were pushed over, as the dogs pulling them crept on their bellies into the wind. When it let up for even a moment, the dogs frantically began to run across the ice. Their sense of smell was keen; if anyone could sniff out the children, it would be the dogs.

The soldiers, silent, moved forward together in their human chain. Even if they had shouted out, you could not have heard them; you could not even have heard your own voice. Suddenly a soldier, Petrov, fell through a hole in the ice cut earlier by the hydraulic engineers! Soaked, he was pulled from the hole, his clothing instantly frozen.

"Get to the hospital," the commander ordered him, shouting through the wind. "Hurry! Just hurry!"

Over and over the radio operators on alert duty sent one question to those in the search parties with radios: "Have you found them?"

"No," came the answer from within the blizzard.

At the boarding school all of the other children knew the boys were missing. They sat at their tables, eating a quiet meal, some eating nothing at all.

Tired of walking up and down the halls waiting, the director of the school started absently toward the boys' room. He was old now; if he had been younger, he would have gone into the blizzard himself. As he stepped into the room, he caught a glimpse of a boot under the bed.

He kicked the boot. It wasn't empty! The director bent down to pull the boot out and pulled out Stas. As Stas crawled back under the bed to finish his dream, the director looked under the next bed, and the next, and the next, pulling one of the missing boys from under each one.

"So," the director said. "What is this all about? What do you have to say for yourselves!"

The boys were still groggy with sleep. They couldn't understand why the director looked so tired, or why his face was so pale. It was Lyonka who said, "It . . . it was all a joke."

"That is some joke." The director sat down on one of the beds and hunched over. "You couldn't have thought of a better one. No, don't take off your coats, we have someplace to go."

On the way the director stopped in his office and telephoned the radio station. Wearily, he told the operator, "We've found the boys . . . asleep under their beds. They thought they were playing a joke."

The radio operator immediately sent a signal out into the blizzard. "The boys have been found! The boys have been found. Asleep, under their beds. It was a joke."

The rescue crew radio operators heard the message and passed it along. Soon all of the search parties were turning back to go home. While there was an ounce of hope, they had fought against the blizzard to find the children; the very sense of anxiety and hope made them double their efforts. Now, they felt tricked, tired and empty. Unfortunately, the blizzard had risen to its worst and wildest point. As they struggled to return, people were struck from all sides by bits of ice and swirling snow, as if the icicles were trying to separate the people from one another, to knock them down and cover their footsteps.

The director led Lyonka, Sanyka, Donyka, and Stas out of his office, and told them to follow him. As they walked down the corridor, all of the other children came out of their rooms and stood there, not saying a word, just looking at the four boys. The director chose four of the older and stronger boys and told each of them to take one of the boys. Just to be sure, he told them to hang onto the younger boys by their collars. And that's how they all went out into the street.

The blizzard wasn't as bad in town as it was on the sound. Besides, they didn't have very far to go. They crossed the street and came to where the director was taking them: the hospital.

There the doctors were busily treating the soldier Petrov. He had been frozen inside his wet clothing, so frozen that he had barely made it back to the hospital. But there were other people in the hospital besides the soldier Petrov. Some had frozen faces, some suffered from frostbite of the hands.

"Here you are, my friends, these are the boys," said the director. "Let them answer to you."

"It was a joke," whispered Lyonka to the faces looking at him. Sanyka and Donyka stood facing away, tears running down their cheeks. The only sound was the doctors quietly speaking to the nurses. There was work to be done.

Translated by Zora Essman

Radii Pogodin

Radii Pogodin was born in 1925. He has been writing for children since 1955. His collection of short stories entitled Of Jolly People and Fine Weather *was translated into English and published by Progress Publishers in 1980.*

THE TREASURE OF LEMON BROWN

Walter Dean Myers

THE DARK SKY, filled with angry, swirling clouds, reflected Greg Ridley's mood as he sat on the stoop of his building. His father's voice came to him again, first reading the letter the principal had sent to the house, then lecturing endlessly about his poor efforts in math.

"I had to leave school when I was thirteen," his father had said, "that's a year younger than you are now. If I'd had half the chances that you have, I'd . . ."

Greg had sat in the small, pale green kitchen listening, knowing the lecture would end with his father saying he couldn't play ball with the Scorpions. He had asked his father the week before, and his father had said it depended on his next report card. It wasn't often the Scorpions took on new players, especially fourteen-year-olds, and this was a chance of a lifetime for Greg. He hadn't been allowed to play high school ball, which he had really wanted to do, but playing for the Community Center team was the next best thing. Report cards were due in a week, and Greg had been hoping for the best. But the principal had ended the suspense early when she sent that letter saying Greg would probably fail math if he didn't spend more time studying.

"And you want to play *basketball?*" His father's brows knitted over deep brown eyes. "That must be some kind of a joke. Now you just get into your room and hit those books."

That had been two nights before. His father's words, like the distant thunder that now echoed through the streets of Harlem, still rumbled softly in his ears.

It was beginning to cool. Gusts of wind made bits of paper dance between the parked cars. There was a flash of nearby lightning, and soon large drops of rain splashed onto his jeans. He stood to go upstairs, thought of the lecture that probably awaited him if he did anything except shut himself in his room with his math book, and started walking down the street instead. Down the block there was an old tenement that had been abandoned for some months. Some of the guys had held an impromptu checker tournament there the week before, and Greg had noticed that the door, once boarded over, had been slightly ajar.

Pulling his collar up as high as he could, he checked for traffic and made a dash across the street. He reached the house just as another flash of lightning changed the night to day for an instant, then returned the graffiti-scarred building to the grim shadows. He vaulted over the outer stairs and pushed tentatively on the door. It was open, and he let himself in.

The inside of the building was dark except for the dim light that filtered through the dirty windows from the streetlamps. There was a room a few feet from the door, and from where he stood at the entrance, Greg could see a squarish patch of light on the floor. He entered the room, frowning at the musty smell. It was a large room that might have been someone's parlor at one time. Squinting, Greg could see an old table on its side against one wall, what looked like a pile of rags or a torn mattress in the corner, and a couch, with one side broken, in front of the window.

He went to the couch. The side that wasn't broken was comfortable enough, though a little creaky. From this spot he could see the blinking neon sign over the bodega on the corner. He sat awhile, watching the sign blink first green then red, allowing his mind to drift to the Scorpions, then to his father. His father had been a postal worker for all Greg's life, and was proud of it, often telling Greg how hard he had worked to pass the test. Greg had heard the story too many times to be interested now.

For a moment Greg thought he heard something that sounded like a scraping against the wall. He listened carefully, but it was gone.

Outside the wind had picked up, sending the rain against the window with a force that shook the glass in its frame. A car passed, its tires hissing over the wet street and its red taillights glowing in the darkness.

Greg thought he heard the noise again. His stomach tightened as he held himself still and listened intently. There weren't any more scraping noises, but he was sure he had heard something in the darkness–something breathing!

He tried to figure out just where the breathing was coming from; he knew it was in the room with him. Slowly he stood, tensing. As he turned, a flash of lightning lit up the room, frightening him with its sudden brilliance. He saw nothing, just the overturned table, the pile of rags and an old newspaper on the floor. Could he have been imagining the sounds? He continued listening, but heard nothing and thought that it might have just been rats. Still, he thought, as soon as the rain let up he would leave. He went to the window and was about to look out when he heard a voice behind him.

"Don't try nothin' 'cause I got a razor here sharp enough to cut a week into nine days!"

Greg, except for an involuntary tremor in his knees, stood stock still. The voice was high and brittle, like dry twigs being broken, surely not one he had ever heard before. There was a shuffling sound as the person who had been speaking moved a step closer. Greg turned, holding his breath, his eyes straining to see in the dark room.

The upper part of the figure before him was still in darkness. The lower half was in the dim rectangle of light that fell unevenly from the window. There were two feet, in cracked, dirty shoes from which rose legs that were wrapped in rags.

"Who are you?" Greg hardly recognized his own voice.

"I'm Lemon Brown," came the answer. "Who're you?"

"Greg Ridley."

"What you doing here?" The figure shuffled forward again, and Greg took a small step backward.

"It's raining," Greg said.

"I can see that," the figure said.

The person who called himself Lemon Brown peered forward, and Greg could see him clearly. He was an old man. His black, heavily wrinkled face was surrounded by a halo of crinkly white hair and whiskers that seemed to separate his head from the layers of dirty coats piled on his smallish frame. His pants were bagged to the knee, where they were met with rags that went down to the old shoes. The rags were held on with strings, and there was a rope around his middle. Greg relaxed. He had seen the man before, picking through the trash on the corner and pulling clothes out of a Salvation Army box. There was no sign of the razor that could "cut a week into nine days."

"What are you doing here?" Greg asked.

"This is where I'm staying," Lemon Brown said. "What you here for?"

"Told you it was raining out," Greg said, leaning against the back of the couch until he felt it give slightly.

"Ain't you got no home?"

"I got a home," Greg answered.

"You ain't one of them bad boys looking for my treasure, is you?" Lemon Brown cocked his head to one side and squinted one eye. "Because I told you I got me a razor."

"I'm not looking for your treasure," Greg answered, smiling. "*If* you have one."

"What you mean, *if* I have one," Lemon Brown said. "Every man got a treasure. You don't know that, you must be a fool!"

"Sure," Greg said as he sat on the sofa and put one leg over the back. "What do you have, gold coins?"

"Don't worry none about what I got," Lemon Brown said. "You know who I am?"

"You told me your name was orange or lemon or something like that."

"Lemon Brown," the old man said, pulling back his shoulders as he did so, "they used to call me Sweet Lemon Brown."

"Sweet Lemon?" Greg asked.

"Yessir. Sweet Lemon Brown. They used to say I sung the blues so sweet that if I sang at a funeral, the dead would commence to rocking with the beat. Used to travel all over Mississippi and as far as Monroe, Louisiana, and east on over to Macon, Georgia. You mean you ain't never heard of Sweet Lemon Brown?"

"Afraid not," Greg said. "What . . . what happened to you?"

"Hard times, boy. Hard times always after a poor man. One day I got tired, sat down to rest a spell and felt a tap on my shoulder. Hard times caught up with me."

"Sorry about that."

"What you doing here? How come you didn't go on home when the rain come? Rain don't bother you young folks none."

"Just didn't." Greg looked away.

"I used to have a knotty-headed boy just like you." Lemon Brown had half walked, half shuffled back to the corner and sat down against the wall. "Had them big eyes like you got. I used to call them moon eyes. Look into them moon eyes and see anything you want."

"How come you gave up singing the blues?" Greg asked.

"Didn't give it up," Lemon Brown said. "You don't give up the blues; they give you up. After a while you do good for yourself, and it ain't nothing but foolishness singing about how hard you got it. Ain't that right?"

"I guess so."

"What's that noise?" Lemon Brown asked, suddenly sitting upright.

Greg listened, and he heard a noise outside. He looked at Lemon Brown and saw the old man was pointing toward the window.

Greg went to the window and saw three men, neighborhood thugs, on the stoop. One was carrying a length of pipe. Greg looked back toward Lemon Brown, who moved quietly across the room to the window. The old man looked out, then beckoned frantically for Greg to follow him. For a moment Greg couldn't move. Then he found himself following Lemon Brown into the hallway and up darkened stairs. Greg followed as closely as he could. They reached the top of the stairs, and Greg felt Lemon Brown's hand first lying on his shoulder, then probing down his arm until he finally took Greg's hand into his own as they crouched in the darkness.

"They's bad men," Lemon Brown whispered. His breath was warm against Greg's skin.

"Hey! Rag man!" A voice called. "We know you in here. What you got up under them rags? You got any money?"

Silence.

"We don't want to have to come in and hurt you, old man, but we don't mind if we have to."

Lemon Brown squeezed Greg's hand in his own hard, gnarled fist.

There was a banging downstairs and a light as the men entered. They banged around noisily, calling for the rag man.

"We heard you talking about your treasure." The voice was slurred. "We just want to see it, that's all."

"You sure he's here?" One voice seemed to come from the room with the sofa.

"Yeah, he stays here every night."

"There's another room over there; I'm going to take a look. You got that flashlight?"

"Yeah, here, take the pipe too."

Greg opened his mouth to quiet the sound of his breath as he sucked it in uneasily. A beam of light hit the wall a few feet opposite him, then went out.

"Ain't nobody in that room," a voice said. "You think he gone or something?"

"I don't know," came the answer. "All I know is that I heard him talking about some kind of treasure. You know they found that shopping bag lady with that money in her bags."

"Yeah. You think he's upstairs?"

"HEY, OLD MAN, ARE YOU UP THERE?"

Silence.

"Watch my back, I'm going up."

There was a footstep on the stairs, and the beam from the flashlight danced crazily along the peeling wallpaper. Greg held his breath. There was another step and a loud crashing noise as the man banged the pipe against the wooden banister. Greg could feel his temples throb as the man slowly neared them. Greg thought about the pipe, wondering what he would do when the man reached them—what he *could* do.

Then Lemon Brown released his hand and moved toward the top of the stairs. Greg looked around and saw stairs going up to the next floor. He tried waving to Lemon Brown, hoping the old man would see him in the dim light and follow him to the next floor. Maybe, Greg thought, the man wouldn't follow them up there.

Suddenly, though, Lemon Brown stood at the top of the stairs, both arms raised high above his head.

"There he is!" A voice cried from below.

"Throw down your money, old man, so I won't have to bash your head in!"

Lemon Brown didn't move. Greg felt himself near panic. The steps came closer, and still Lemon Brown didn't move. He was an eerie sight, a bundle of rags standing at the top of the stairs, his shadow on the wall looming over him. Maybe, the thought came to Greg, the scene could be even eerier.

Greg wet his lips, put his hands to his mouth and tried to make a sound. Nothing came out. He swallowed hard, wet his lips once more and howled as evenly as he could.

"*What's that?*"

As Greg howled, the light moved away from Lemon Brown, but not before Greg saw him hurl his body down the stairs at the men who had come to take his treasure. There was a crashing noise, and then footsteps. A rush of warm air came in as the downstairs door opened, then there was only an ominous silence.

Greg stood on the landing. He listened, and after a while there was another sound on the staircase.

"Mr. Brown?" he called.

"Yeah, it's me," came the answer. "I got their flashlight."

Greg exhaled in relief as Lemon Brown made his way slowly back up the stairs.

"You OK?"

"Few bumps and bruises," Lemon Brown said.

"I think I'd better be going," Greg said, his breath returning to normal. "You'd better leave, too, before they come back."

"They may hang around outside for a while," Lemon Brown said, "but they ain't getting their nerve up to come in here again. Not with crazy old rag men and howling spooks. Best you stay a while till the coast is clear. I'm heading out west tomorrow, out to east St. Louis."

"They were talking about treasures," Greg said. "You *really* have a treasure?"

"What I tell you? Didn't I tell you every man got a treasure?" Lemon Brown said. "You want to see mine?"

"If you want to show it to me," Greg shrugged.

"Let's look out the window first, see what them scoundrels be doing," Lemon Brown said.

They followed the oval beam of the flashlight into one of the rooms and looked out the window. They saw the men who had tried to take the treasure sitting on the curb near the corner. One of them had his pants leg up, looking at his knee.

"You sure you're not hurt?" Greg asked Lemon Brown.

"Nothing that ain't been hurt before," Lemon Brown said. "When you get as old as me all you say when something hurts is, 'Howdy, Mr. Pain, sees you back again.' Then when Mr. Pain see he can't worry you none, he go on mess with somebody else."

Greg smiled.

"Here, you hold this." Lemon Brown gave Greg the flashlight.

He sat on the floor near Greg and carefully untied the strings that held the rags on his right leg. When he took the rags away, Greg saw a piece of plastic. The old man carefully took off the plastic and unfolded it. He revealed some yellowed newspaper clippings and a battered harmonica.

"There it be," he said, nodding his head. "There it be."

Greg looked at the old man, saw the distant look in his eye, then turned to the clippings. They told of Sweet Lemon Brown, a blues singer and harmonica player who was appearing at different theaters in the South. One of the clippings said he had been the hit of the show, although not the headliner. All of the clippings were reviews of shows Lemon Brown had been in more than 50 years ago. Greg looked at the harmonica. It was dented badly on one side, with the reed holes on one end nearly closed.

"I used to travel around and make money for to feed my wife and Jesse—that's my boy's name. Used to feed them good, too. Then his mama died, and he stayed with his mama's sister. He growed up to be a man, and when the war come he saw fit to go off and fight in it. I didn't have nothing to give him except these things that told him who I was, and what he come from. If you know your pappy did something, you know you can do something too.

"Anyway, he went off to war, and I went off still playing and singing. 'Course by then I wasn't as much as I used to be, not without somebody to make it worth the while. You know what I mean?"

"Yeah," Greg nodded, not quite really knowing.

"I traveled around, and one time I come home, and there was this letter saying Jesse got killed in the war. Broke my heart, it truly did.

"They sent back what he had with him over there, and what it was is this old mouth fiddle and these clippings. Him carrying it around with him like that told me it meant something to him. That was my treasure, and when I give it to him he treated it just like that, a treasure. Ain't that something?"

"Yeah, I guess so," Greg said.

"You *guess* so?" Lemon Brown's voice rose an octave as he started to put his treasure back into the plastic. "Well, you got to guess 'cause you sure don't know nothing. Don't know enough to get home when it's raining."

"I guess . . . I mean, you're right."

"You OK for a youngster," the old man said as he tied the strings around his leg, "better than those scalawags what come here looking for my treasure. That's for sure."

"You really think that treasure of yours was worth fighting for?" Greg asked. "Against a pipe?"

"What else a man got 'cepting what he can pass on to his son, or his daughter, if she be his oldest?" Lemon Brown said. "For a big-headed boy you sure do ask the foolishest questions."

Lemon Brown got up after patting his rags in place and looked out the window again.

"Looks like they're gone. You get on out of here and get yourself home. I'll be watching from the window so you'll be all right."

Lemon Brown went down the stairs behind Greg. When they reached the front door the old man looked out first, saw the street was clear and told Greg to scoot on home.

"You sure you'll be OK?" Greg asked.

"Now didn't I tell you I was going to east St. Louis in the morning?" Lemon Brown asked. "Don't that sound OK to you?"

"Sure it does," Greg said. "Sure it does. And you take care of that treasure of yours."

"That I'll do," Lemon said, the wrinkles about his eyes suggesting a smile. "That I'll do."

The night had warmed and the rain had stopped, leaving puddles at the curbs. Greg didn't even want to think how late it was. He thought ahead of what his father would say and wondered if he should tell him about Lemon Brown. He thought about it until he reached his stoop, and decided against it. Lemon Brown would be OK, Greg thought, with his memories and his treasure.

Greg pushed the button over the bell marked Ridley, thought of the lecture he knew his father would give him, and smiled.

Walter Dean Myers

Walter Dean Myers was born in 1937 in West Virginia. A graduate of Empire State College, he was a senior trade books editor and taught creative writing and black history before turning to writing full time. He is commonly recognized as one of modern literature's premier authors of fiction for young black people and is best known for his novels that explore the lives of young Harlem blacks. He is equally adept at producing modern fairy tales, ghost stories, and adventure sagas. He has won the Coretta Scott King Award twice, for his books The Young Landlords *and* Motown and Didi: A Love Story, *the American Library Association "Best Books for Young Adults" citation several times, and the Council on Interracial Books for Children Award. He and his family live in Jersey City, New Jersey,* USA.

FORTUNE'S FAVORITE

Gunars Cirulis

PAVILS, SWITCH off the TV set and go to bed, it's high time, there'll be no waking you in the morning again," Grandma called from her room. She didn't sound very imperative, or confident of prompt obedience, but with both of Pavils's parents out it was up to Grandma to implement domestic discipline. You had to have some sort of order in the home!

"All right, just a minute, Gran," Pavils called back casually from his comfortable seat in a deep armchair; as usual, he sounded quite unruffled. "I'll just wait and see the numbers drawn in the sport-lotto."

It was a long time since he had believed in the possibility of a decent win, but all the same he still bought a card every week and filled it in, just as practically all the other kids at school did. At first he had had a system—or, rather, several; he had marked the numbers of his favourite games or athletics, or the family birthdays; sometimes he had followed arithmetical progression. His father and younger sister had shared in the weighty proceedings. Their advice was very valuable, of course, but all the same he could boast only the unique record of never hitting a winning number. Gradually his interest waned; nowadays he marked the numbers as chance dictated, not bothering about any kind of ingenious system. Strange as it might seem he had better luck that way. Five times running he had guessed two numbers, and the last time it would have been three if his hand hadn't trembled so that instead of free-style wrestling he crossed out the very similar classical wrestling. Alberts, who shared a double desk with Pavils, had twice won three roubles. But he was a fanatic, he always bought six tickets.

Pavils increased the sound and was just about to get his sport-lotto card from his schoolbag when Grandma called again.

"Pavils, take my card, too, and see if I've won anything. Maybe fortune's smiled on a rickety old woman. That would be my lucky day!"

Lucky all right–more like a miracle, thought Pavils when he saw Grandma's card. Apparently the old woman had thought this card was no different from an ordinary lottery ticket and hadn't even filled it in, let alone cutting off the necessary part. She had simply bought it and slipped it under the cushion where she kept her pension book, the decoration awarded her late husband, newspaper cuttings with advice from doctors and various other treasures. For a whole week Grandma had kept her secret and waited patiently to see whether luck had brought her something really big, so that she could go to a sanatorium and treat her rheumatism.

Pavils didn't know whether he should tell her or not. No, that would upset her too much, better let her think that she had lost because her luck was out, not through her own fault. It's easier for old people to resign themselves to plain bad luck.

When Pavils returned to the dining room the transparent drum was already revolving on the screen and the plastic balls were dancing, jumping up, falling back and whirling frantically in the magic circle as though trying to escape. In vain! The drum slowed and stopped, the mechanical arm reached into the thick of the balls, grabbed several and sent the first rolling down the transparent tunnel. The ball bore a number: 10.

"Iceboating!" the commentator announced with casual indifference. His comments on hockey matches were very different!

Pavils pulled a face. He didn't remember which numbers he had crossed out on his own card but it certainly would never have entered his head to mark a sport which didn't attract him. To keep the number in mind he crossed out the "10" on Grandma's card.

The balls were dancing again: just as before they jostled, jumping aside as though they were trying to break out of their cage; but they were compelled to submit to the established order, and only one was freed, number 13.

"Sailing! Gosh–it's crazy! Not a scrap of logic!" shouted Pavils in deep disgust–as though you could expect logic in a lottery!

Other balls followed–28, 41, 36.

At last Pavils got his own card out of his school bag. Not a single winning number yet!

The last result of his chance selection was a five, the only number marked on Pavils's card.

For some time he stared at Grandma's card where six squares were now filled in with crosses. What on earth had stopped him from marking those squares two days ago! He took the pen and crossed over those numbers on the B part too. So simple and easy! Imagination seized control, for a moment he pretended to himself that the drawing was still ahead, that some magic power had made it possible for him to foresee the winning numbers. He wrote them in the upper part of the card, creased it and tore it neatly. Oh, if only he'd written them two days ago, instead of those other damfool numbers, he'd have been receiving five thousand roubles in a week's time! And then Gran–she'd probably have stubbornly refused at first but she'd have given in and gone to the Black Sea, Dad would have bought a Jawa motor-bike and stopped having to hunt all up and down town for spare parts for his prehistoric Izhik, then he'd have bought a color TV set, and for him. . .Pavils crushed the card angrily and hurled it into the wastepaper basket. He had been dreaming of a motor-bike for so long a time, it had come to mean so much, that it was impossible to think of it as a mere daydream.

Pavils slammed his textbook shut without a glance at the material set. He and Andris would be absent from the first lesson anyway, they were to train at the school rifle range. The history teacher had been informed, so there was no danger of getting a bad mark.

Bad luck still pursued him the next day. The sports master did not come; he had left a box of airgun bullets and a note urging both the team marksmen to train seriously. However, before the boys had done more than make a beginning, the cleaner appeared armed with bucket, broom and swabs.

"I don't know anything about your training and care less!" the sharp-tongued old woman declared when she heard the boys' laments; she had worked at the school ever since the war and considered herself the mistress. "Tomorrow there's repairs and decorating beginning here, and nobody but the headmaster can change that, so if you don't like it you'd better go and complain to him."

Naturally, they didn't. They pocketed the bullets and lounged about the stairs and corridors until break. To go into the classroom in the middle of the lesson would have been sheer lunacy, for the history teacher recognized only the antique Olympian games and regarded modern sports as the invention of idlers with the one object of missing lessons.

The bell rang for break but the classroom door remained shut. Was it possible that even after the bell she couldn't break off her talk about Napoleon's invasion and the Battle of Berezina? She would have been telling them again not to think it was enough to see the film, they must read Lev Tolstoy's *War and Peace*.

At last the teacher did emerge. Seeing Pavils, she smiled acidly. "Go in, fortune's favorite! Only remember: greed has ruined many outstanding people!"

Inside the room, too, a surprise awaited him. Barely had he crossed the threshold than Alberts raised his hand, and there was a chorus of "Congratulations, lucky boy, we wish you all the greatest joy!"

"Hey, what's got into you all? It isn't my birthday!" Pavils protested.

"No, but you are the third person in the republic to get all six numbers!" cried Alberts, waving the clipping from the sport-lotto card which he had found in Pavils's history book. "Say, Pavils, how much of it d'you think your parents'll let you keep?"

Pavils felt himself turning red, even his ears were hot. That kid's game he had fooled about with the previous evening would make him the laughingstock of the class. It hadn't seemed particularly daft at the time–sitting in the cozy semidarkness at home, letting himself dream, seeing himself for a brief moment as a millionaire. But now, in the hard light of day, he felt desperately ashamed of dreams that were so miserably petty. He could have hit himself, but to expose his own silliness to the whole class–for that his courage failed him. He'd try to play for time, wriggle out until the sensation wasn't so fresh and startling. Pavils knew his classmates, the fame of his wealth would quickly be forgotten. Five thousand roubles couldn't occupy them for long.

"Why, of course, the drawing was yesterday!" His pretence of forgetfulness came out quite naturally. "Only hope my kid sister didn't forget to post the card. Why, have I really guessed some of the numbers?"

"Not just some, all six of them!" Alberts's excitement grew. "We're the first to congratulate you, so you have to treat us. After school we'll go to Luna Park."

"I'd treat you all right, but I haven't a kopeck to do it with." Pavils felt an enormous relief at getting off so easily.

"Doesn't matter, your credit's good." Alberts had no intention of postponing such an attractive prospect. "Hey, kids, turn out your pockets. How much has everyone got?"

Luna Park greeted them with three melodies simultaneously. Fortunately they were all good old twists, otherwise the cacophony would have been crazy. But strange as it might seem, the closer they got, the less irritating the music seemed.

As usually happens when a whole group plans to do something, half the seventh form had drifted away before they ever left the school. Some had to go for training, others were due at hobby circles, yet others were expected at home and Laimonis, nicknamed The Model, said that they ought to do their homework first and then think of amusements. On the way to the park a cold wind suddenly got up bringing with it stinging rain; this sent several of the girls home, so that only a baker's dozen arrived at their objective, Alberts and the Twelve Thieves, as they dubbed themselves, for they planned, as they said, to "make a cleanup at all the games."

However, the first steps showed that they were more likely to find themselves cleaned out, and that, fast. They wandered off separately because each one wanted to try his luck at the automatic machines (one-armed bandits!) and at the lottery. The money in Alberts's games bag melted away with alarming rapidity. Something had to be done before they were quite bankrupt.

Alberts gathered them all behind the Chamber of Horrors, out of the wind, and delivered a speech.

"Up to now we've only squandered money like old-time peasants having a high old time in the city. We've got to think how we can restore material values, otherwise we'll soon be as bare as unemployed in Sahara."

"What if we pawn Pavils's ticket?" Andris suggested.

"Don't talk daft! They'd think we're crooks and take it off us. No, we've got to earn money with cool brains and skilled hands!" Alberts had definitely assumed the role of leader. "That's settled, then–the rest of our small change we're going to spend only where we can win something."

"At 'flippers,' with eight hundred thousand points you can win a three-rouble German doll," said Janis, the school champion in athletics.

"That's more like it! We'll sell it right away for two. Take Inna and do your stuff!"

"But I want to go in the Chamber of Horrors," Inna said, pouting. "Mum says you have to take validol when you go. Skeletons pull your hair and a spectre wanted to sit on her knee–"

"You don't need to pay for that," Pavils teased. "I'll give you such a fright in any dark corridor that you'll dream of spectres for three nights after."

"It isn't fair," Andris objected in his turn. "You went on the electric carts, why shouldn't I?"

"Wait a bit, when we go home the trolleybus'll give you as good a shake-up for only four kopecks. But for sixty we can have three goes at the shooting gallery."

"And win a model of one of those vintage cars. Collectors won't grudge three roubles for that," said Sandra. She had four brothers and was regarded as a technical expert.

"Smashing!" Alberts said with high approval. "We've two marksmen from the school team. So look out, you there at the gallery, we're coming!"

"I wouldn't soil my hands with those crooked-bores," Andris declared. "They've corkscrews for sights! By the time you've got your eye in and learnt their tricks you've shot away all your money!"

Pavils thought the same. Skilled shots felt it beneath them to demonstrate their skill at fun fairs, where they might expect all kinds of tricks. However, this time he had no choice. He was hardly likely to come across another chance to get back his friends' money and please them at the same time.

But what if he disgraced himself? Wouldn't that be even worse than disclosure of his unintentional joke with Grandma's card? No, only he was to blame for that card, but for a failure at the shooting gallery he could blame the gun. Besides, there was another possibility: people must hit a bull's-eye *sometimes.*

Anyway, it was too late to draw back. Leons, who always followed Alberts's lead without a second thought, was already by the paydesk waving the tickets he'd just bought.

The targets seemed nearly close enough to touch; the thin sticks almost like reeds which the bullets must break were only a few metres from the barrier; it was just this which aroused Pavils's mistrust. The expensive nature of the prizes did the same. They were probably calculated to make greed win over caution, so that people would keep on spending more and more money.

The abundance of prizes was certainly fascinating. Model cars, lighters, cowboy belts and penknives, packets of chewing gum and magnificent dolls. The girls eyed some crystal vases–he needed only twelve successful shots to win one.

Pavils knew there must be a trick somewhere, otherwise those girls in jeans wouldn't have been looking at the people outside the barrier so superciliously.

You'd think there was nothing in it. Lift the gun, take aim and pull the trigger.

The crack of shots seemed practically continuous but the grove of sticks got no thinner. Only one marksman managed at the fourth try to hit four sticks and receive a box of peppermints which he ceremoniously presented to his girlfriend.

"No sense in being stingy; if we're going to risk it, then risk the lot!" Alberts whispered excitedly. "That vintage Tatra's just what we want."

It was certainly a beautiful model, rather touching with its old-fashioned, impractical features–its wire wheels, its outside gear lever and its wide-mouthed horn. It would really be a shame to sell it! But first they had to win it, and that meant hitting the five sticks underneath.

"It's not permitted to support your elbows on the barrier," the girl warned them–so pleasantly that they wanted to thank her, as though she had given them good advice.

Alberts took on the role of assistant and dropped the first bullet in the barrel.

"Go to it!"

The air gun looked very little different from an ordinary rifle. The butt against his shoulder and the breech ring against his cheek were comfortably familiar, and Pavils felt happier. He drew a deep breath, took a stick in the sight, let out his breath and pressed the trigger.

There was a quiet pop and the first stick broke. Pavils had time to see that the bullet had hit the left side, evidently the gun carried slightly left, he must take that into consideration.

He tried to drive out all disturbing thoughts–about his classmates crowding excitedly around, about the prize which he simply *must* win, about the reason why he was standing here in the shooting gallery trembling over every kopeck. Could Alberts possibly have persuaded Eva to dip into the Komsomol fund of the class? Impossible–she'd sooner put in her own money to cover any shortage. Only–how had they managed to scrape together so much? Stop it–no sense distracting himself, he had to concentrate on the target. There it was, no thicker than a match–now get it in the sight.

A shot. Crack. A sigh of relief from the kids followed by exclamations of satisfaction.

"Here–load and shoot!" Alberts handed him the next bullet.

After the third hit the girl in charge (for some reason he liked to fancy that she was the daughter of the proprietor and dreamed of a better job) smiled at Pavils, and after the fourth became quite eager for him to win.

"Go on–one more and the model is yours!"

Pavils gripped the air gun and prepared for the final shot. He'd show them what a Riga lad could do! He was just about to pull the trigger when the girl abruptly turned away to serve another customer. But it was too late to stop himself. There was a "pop" and the bullet went wide.

He didn't believe his eyes. He stared at the one lonely stick, at the model which he had already regarded as his. Of all the luck!

He heard Alberts's excited whisper.

"Don't stand there like a gawk, take this and shoot!"

It was only some time later when his trembling hand already held the beautifully packed Tatra that Pavils understood that the last bullet must have come from Alberts's pocket. Of course he could have raised a row, exposed Alberts's cheating, but then he would have had to take the step logically following, admit his own dishonesty, admit that the whole visit to Luna Park was based on a misunderstanding, that he was no favourite of fortune but only a silly ass who'd been pretending to himself like some daft kid that he'd won the sport-lotto. But maybe it would be better not to explain anything, simply refuse the prize? But wouldn't that mean letting down his comrades who'd been so glad about it? No, no, later on he'd find a way to get himself out of this horrible muddle, but now he must look as if nothing was wrong. Was it his fault if for the second time that day he'd found himself forced into deceit!

Janis and Inna returned. Even when they were some distance away it was clear from their expressions that they had failed.

"You know–with the first go I won two extra balls," said Janis. "And before the last I had nearly got eight hundred thousand points. And then–I just can't understand how it happened, but the last ball slipped out of my hand. I was almost there–almost–"

"You can put up your 'almost' on the Board of Honour at school," snapped Alberts angrily. "What's up with you, Inna? Turning on the waterworks?"

Inna managed to swallow her tears, although her voice trembled suspiciously.

"What do you want? Shout hurrah? I've spent everything to the last kopeck. And it's my parents' wedding anniversary today, Dad gave me ten roubles this morning to get a present for mum."

"Why didn't you say so? We needn't have rolled those daft balls!" As though twenty kopecks could have saved the situation.

"You think I didn't want to, myself?" Inna was ready to cry again.

Pavils felt worse than anybody. Of course, it was good that they hadn't touched the membership dues, but that didn't make his own fault any less. He stepped forward and spoke uncertainly.

"Could you give your mother this model? It's a pity to sell it–it's awful pretty."

Inna smiled wryly.

"Thanks–but it's a long time since my mother played with toys."

Then Alberts spoke. It was at such times that he hit upon ideas which fully justified his fame as a leader.

"There isn't a woman on earth who wouldn't be pleased to get a crystal vase. Another good try and we'll have your present."

"But where'll we get the money?" Andris remembered. "We'd have to buy twelve tickets."

"We'll try and persuade the woman to take tram coupons," Sandra suggested. "I've got a whole sixty kopeck book of them."

The others, too, had coupons and Leons even found some coins in the lining of his jacket, so Alberts set out on his diplomatic mission.

Nobody knew how he managed to talk the rather grim woman at

the pay desk around, but the result proved his persuasiveness. He showed himself farsighted, too–he asked the girl for the same gun Pavils had used before.

The first six bullets broke six sticks. But only Pavils himself realized how great his luck was–it could happen only once in a lifetime that the seventh bullet should not only hit the seventh stick but actually break the eighth alongside it, too! But his hand trembled during the ninth try. However, he went on shooting and his success returned. Only one stick still stood under the crystal vase. But his bullets were finished.

Suddenly Pavils remembered the school bullets in his jacket pocket. He unfastened his overcoat.

"Quick!" whispered Alberts, guessing his intention.

The illicit bullet was in the barrel but the target danced before the sight. Pavils knew that his hand would regain its steadiness. But–his conscience? He wasn't afraid of being found out, the girl was at the other end of the gallery; he felt a different uncomfortable fear–that this time, too, he would pull off the deception. He was no longer particularly worried by what had happened in the classroom–who'd refuse to march about with a peacock tail? And the trick with the model–well, you could pass that off, too, with a bit of an effort–just a boy's trick. But the vase–that was an expensive thing. Wouldn't it be just–stealing?

It wasn't only the value of the prize that bothered him; he couldn't help feeling that he had strayed onto the wrong path, onto slippery ground.

Pavils raised the gun and fired into the air. He put the gun back on the barrier. He felt as though after swimming for a long time he had his feet on firm ground. He turned to Inna and spoke almost gaily.

"Come along home with me. Dad bought a pottery vase the day before yesterday, it's really pretty, I know your mother'll like it."

Pavils well knew how difficult it would be to explain to his parents why he just had to have that vase. But he knew, too, that it was the only thing to do.

Translated by Eve Manning

Gunars Cirulis

Gunars Cirulis was born in 1923 in Riga. He is a prose writer and scenario writer, the author of numerous novels and collections of essays and a graduate of the Geneva Translators' School. A number of films based on his work have been made at the Riga Film Studio. He has written several adventure books for children, including The "Tobago" Changes Its Course, The Treasure of Form 6 "B", Don't Trust the Stork, *and* Touring Through Ventspils.

TRAFFIC ON SADOVOI ROAD

Victor Dragunsky

VANYKA DIKHOV HAD a bicycle. It was an old bike, but still in pretty good condition. Originally it had been his father's, but one day when the bike broke down, his father said to him, "Here, Vanyka, instead of running around the street all day, take the bike and fix it up. Then you'll have your own bicycle. I bought it a long time ago in a junkyard, but it was almost new then. It might still be good for a while."

It is hard to explain just how happy Vanyka was with that bicycle. He stopped running around; in fact, he did just the opposite. He spent all day fussing with the bicycle. He took it to a corner of the yard and hammered out fenders and tightened screws, and he banged and scraped and painted. More often than not he was covered with machine oil, and his fingers were always bandaged because in hammering he hit his fingers as often as he hit the bicycle.

Even so, the bicycle began to take shape, in part because the fifth-graders all took metal shop and Vanyka was one of the best in class. Often I helped him fix his bike. Every day he would say to me, "Just you wait, Deniska. Once we get it fixed up, I'll take you for a great ride. You can sit on the baggage rack, and you and I'll ride all over Moscow!" And because he was so nice to me, and so friendly even though I am in a younger class, I helped him all the more. Because of his promise to me, I was especially anxious to work on the baggage rack to be sure that it turned out nice. I painted it over four times with black enamel. When it was done, it was really shiny, just like a brand-new car, beautiful and shiny. It was almost as if the baggage rack were my own. It made me so happy to think of how I would ride around on it, holding onto Vanyka's belt, and how he and I would ride around the whole world like that.

Then one day Vanyka lifted the bicycle up from the ground, pumped air into the tires, wiped the whole bicycle clean with a rag, washed himself with water from the barrel, and clamped some white clips onto his trousers. I realized that the great day had come.

Vanyka climbed on his bicycle and rode off. First, he pedaled slowly around our yard. The bike just seemed to glide under him, and you could hear the pleasant hum of the tires rolling across the ground. Then he rode a little faster, and the spokes began to whistle. Vanyka began to do figure eights. Then he went really fast and braked so suddenly the bike stopped as if it were rooted to the ground. He kept checking the bicycle over and over as if he were a test pilot. I just stood there and watched, as if I were the mechanic, watching all the tricks of my great pilot.

I was happy that Vanyka was such a great rider, even though I knew I was a better rider, well, just as good anyway. But the bicycle wasn't mine. It was his, and he should do whatever he wanted to do.

It was nice to see the bike, all shiny and bright from the new paint. In fact, it was hard to guess that it was old. I though it was better than any new bike. Especially the baggage rack. I even loved looking at it.

Anyway, Vanyka rode around like that for more than half an hour. I began to be afraid that he had forgotten about me, but no, I shouldn't have even thought that. After one round, he rode right up to me, leaned his foot against the gate, and said, "Get on."

While I was clambering on, I asked, "Where are we going?"

"What difference does it make?" Vanyka said. "Let's go around the world!"

I was so happy. I felt as if the world were filled with happy people who had nothing to do but wait for Vanyka and me to come and visit them. And once we came to them, Vanyka on the bicycle and me on the baggage rack, there would be big parties and holidays with flags waving and balloons all over, and there would be singing and ice cream sticks for everyone, and brass bands and clowns standing on their heads!

That's how wonderful I felt as I climbed onto my baggage rack and grabbed hold of Vanyka's belt. Vanyka started pedaling. So long, Papa! I thought. Good-bye, Mama. Good-bye, old yard, and pigeons, good-bye to you, too. We're off to ride around the whole wide world.

Vanyka pulled out of the yard, and we were off around the corner, and then down streets I had only walked on before. Everything looked so different now, unfamiliar, and Vanyka kept ringing his bell so he wouldn't hit anyone: rrrrring, rrrrring, rrrrring! The pedestrians jumped out of our way like chickens out of a road, and we kept going at an unbelievable speed. I felt so happy and my heart felt so free; I wanted to shout something wild. So I yelled out, "Ahhhhhhhhhhhhhhhh!"

It was so funny when Vanyka rode down an old cobblestone street. The bike began to shake and my "Ahhhhhhhhhhh" began to sound all broken up, as if as soon as it came out of my mouth, someone cut it off with a knife and threw it into the wind. "Ah . . . Ah . . . Ah . . . Ah . . . Ah!" But then we rode back onto the asphalt, and my voice sounded smooth as butter again: "Ahhhhhhhhhhhhhhhhhhhhhh!"

We rode around all the streets and all the alleys in our neighborhood for a long time, but then we got tired. Vanyka stopped and I jumped down off the baggage rack.

Vanyka said, "So, how was it?"

"Terrific," I said.

"Were you comfortable?"

"Just as if I were on a couch," I said. "Even more comfortable. This is some bike, real class!"

He laughed and smoothed down his hair. His face was dusty and dirty, but his eyes shone bright blue, like the plates hanging on our kitchen wall. And he was all smiles.

And then this strange man came up to us. Tall, with one golden tooth, he wore a striped shirt with long sleeves and had tattoos drawn on his hands—some faces and a landscape. A shaggy little dog hung back behind him. It seemed to be made of different wools, patches of black, some white, an occasional red, even some green patches. Its tail looked like a pretzel, and one leg was shorter than the others.

"Where are you boys from?" the man asked.

"From Trekhprudnaya Street," we answered.

Then he said, "You're pretty good on that bike! Incredible! Is it your bike?"

Vanyka said, "Yes, it's mine. It was my father's, but now it's mine. I fixed it up. This little kid here," he said, pointing to me, "helped me."

"No fooling," said the man. "You're not much to look at, you two, but you're regular mechanics, aren't you?"

Then I said, "Is that your dog?"

He said, "Yep, it's mine. Very valuable. It's a pedigree Spanish dachshund."

Then Vanyka said, "No! What kind of a dachshund is that? Dachshunds are long and thin."

"If you don't know much about something," the man said, "it's better to keep your mouth shut. Moscow or Ryazin dachshunds are long because they spend all their time lying under cabinets; that's why they grow long. This dog is different. He's very valuable, and he's a true friend. Zhulik is his name."

The man was quiet for a moment. Then he sighed three deep sighs and said, "What difference does it make? Even though he's a good animal, he's still just a dog. He can't help me with my troubles. . . ." Tears came to the man's eyes.

My heart sank. What was wrong with him? Worried, Vanyka asked, "What's your trouble?"

The man seemed to stagger, then he leaned against the wall. "My grandmother's dying," he said. He started to gasp for breath, sniffling. "She's dying of . . . double appendicitis." He took a quick look at us and then said, "Double appendicitis . . . and measles, too."

At this point he began to cry very hard, wiping the tears with his sleeve. My heart began to pound. Then the man leaned on the wall and began to howl. His dog took a look at him and began to howl too. So the two of them just stood there and howled. It was horrible to listen to. The howling even made Vanyka turn pale, under all the dust and dirt, that is.

He put his hand on the man's shoulder and with a trembling voice said, "Please, don't cry like that. Why are you crying?"

"How can I not cry?" he said, rolling his head up and down. "How can I not cry when I don't even have strength left to get to the drugstore to help my grandmother? I haven't eaten for three days!"

And the man started howling louder and stronger than ever. So did his valuable dachshund. There was no one anywhere around. I didn't know what to do. But Vanyka didn't lose his cool at all.

"Do you have the prescription?" he shouted. "If you do, give it to me. I'll just get on my bike and ride down to the drugstore and bring you the medicine back. I'll go really fast."

I almost jumped for joy. Vanyka was great. What could ever happen to a person with a friend like this? He always knew just what to do. We'd just ride down to the drugstore and bring this guy his medicine and save his grandmother's life. I shouted, "Give us the prescription. We don't want to lose any time."

But the man stopped howling and, waving his hands at us, yelled, "No, you can't do that! Are you crazy? How could I send two young boys out onto Sadovoi Road? Especially on a bicycle. Do you have any idea of the traffic out there? You'd be torn to shreds in half a second . . . legs one way, hands another, heads somewhere else! There are five-ton trucks out there. Huge cranes go up and down the street. You'd be fine, all right; you'd just be crushed. I'd have to answer for you. I'd be responsible. No, I won't let you go, no matter what you say. Let poor old Granny just die, my poor Fevronia Polukarpovan." He started howling again in his deep bass voice, and his valuable dog started howling again, too.

I couldn't stand it anymore. Imagine this man so good and kind that he was willing to sacrifice his grandmother's life so that nothing would happen to us. My lip began to twitch and I knew that before long I'd be howling worse than the dog.

Even Vanyka's eyes began to tear, and he began to sniffle. "What should we do?"

"It's very simple," said the man, in a very businesslike voice. "There's just one way out. Give me your bicycle. I'll ride down and get the medicine and then I'll come right back. Or may I not be free for a hundred years!" And he drew his finger across his throat—probably some kind of terrible oath. He reached for the bike. But Vanyka had a strong hold on it. The man tried to pull it loose. Then he gave up and started howling again. "Ai, ai, ai, my poor granny is dying for want of a nail. Dying for nothing . . . ai . . . ai . . ." He began pulling his hair, putting his hands on his head and pulling his hair!

I couldn't stand it anymore. I started crying, and I said to Vanyka, "Give him the bicycle. His grandmother will die. What if it were your grandmother?" Vanyka held onto the cycle and crying said, "No, it's better if I go myself." That's when the man looked at Vanyka with his wild eyes and growled like a crazy person, "You don't trust me, right? You don't believe me? You won't give me your silly wheels for just a moment? Let the old lady die. Right? Poor old lady in her white kerchief, let her die from the measles. The brave adventurer with the red kerchief who won't give up his silly wheels, for a few minutes, that's you. Murderers! Privateers!"

He tore a button off his shirt and began stamping on it. We didn't move. We were all cried out, Vanyka and I. Then, all of a sudden, this guy picked up his valuable dachshund from the ground, and started shoving it first into my arms and then into Vanyka's. "Here. Here, I'll give you my best friend as a deposit, my very best friend I'll give to you. Now do you believe me? I'm giving you this valuable dog, this pedigree dachshund." Somehow he managed to shove the dog into Vanyka's arms.

That's when it dawned on me. I said, "Vanyka, he's leaving us his dog as a hostage. Where could he possibly go without his best friend, and such a valuable friend? Give him the bike. Don't worry."

So Vanyka handed the bike over to this man and said, "Is fifteen minutes enough for you?"

"More than enough," the man said. "Five minutes should do it. Wait for me here. Don't move from this spot!" He jumped smoothly onto the machine and took right off, turning into Sadovoi Road.

Just as he turned into the main street, though, that valuable dog suddenly jumped out of Vanyka's arms and ran after the man like a bolt of lightning.

Vanyka yelled out to me, "Grab him!"

But what could I do? "I can never catch up with him," I said. "He's run after his master. He's lost without him! That's what a best friend means, Vanyka. I only wish I had one like that."

"But isn't he our hostage?" Vanyka asked timidly. "Our deposit."

"Don't worry," I said. "They'll both be back soon."

We waited five minutes.

"They don't seem to be back yet," Vanyka said.

"There must have been a long wait at the drugstore," I said.

Almost two more hours passed, but the man never showed up. Neither did his dog. When it began to grow dark, Vanyka took me by the hand. "It's all clear to me now," he said. "Let's go home."

"What's clear to you, Vanyka?" I asked.

"What a fool, I am. What a fool," Vanyka said. "He won't be back. Never, not that crook. Neither will my bicycle, or the valuable dachshund."

Vanyka never said another word about that day. Maybe he didn't want me to think about it. But I thought of it anyway. There really is a lot of traffic on Sadovoi Road.

Translated by Zora Essman

Victor Dragunsky

Victor Dragunsky (1913–1972), a Russian writer and actor, was born in New York. His first work appeared in print in 1940. He wrote numerous humoristic stories, sketches, and scenes for variety theater. In 1959 he started writing stories for children, under the general title Deniska's Stories. *He spent most of his life in Moscow.*

THE BOY WHO DREW UNICORNS

Jane Yolen

THERE WAS ONCE a boy who drew unicorns. Even before he knew their names, he caught them mane and hoof and horn on his paper. And they were white beasts and gray, black beasts and brown, galloping across the brown supermarket bags. He didn't know what to call them at first, but he knew what they called him: Phillip, a lover of horses, Philly, Phil.

Now, children, there is going to be a new boy in class today. His name is Philadelphia Carew.

Philadelphia? That's a city name not a kid's name.

Hey, my name is New York.

Call me Chicago.

I got a cousin named India, does that count?

Enough, children. This young man is very special. You must try to be kind to him. He'll be very shy. And he's had a lot of family problems.

I got family problems too, Ms. Wynne. I got a brother and he's a big *problem.*

Joseph, that's enough.

He's six feet tall. That's a very big problem.

Now you may all think you have problems, but this young man has more than most. You see, he doesn't talk.

Not ever?

No. Not now. Not for several years. That's close enough to ever, I think.

Bet you'd like it if we didn't talk. Not for several years.

No, I wouldn't like that at all, though if I could shut you up for several hours, Joseph . . .

Oooooh, Joey, she's got you!

"What is the good of such drawing, Philadelphia?" his mother said. "If you have to draw, draw something useful. Draw me some money or some groceries or a new man, one who doesn't beat us. Draw us some better clothes or a bed for yourself. Draw me a job."

But he drew only unicorns: horse-like, goat-like, deer-like, lamb-like, bull-like, things he had seen in books. Four-footed, silken swift, with the single golden horn. His corner of the apartment was papered with them.

When's he coming, Ms. Wynne?

Today. After lunch.

Does he look weird, too?

He's not weird, Joseph. He's special. And I expect you—all of you—to act special.

She means we shouldn't talk.

No, Joseph, I mean you *need to think before you talk. Think what it must be like not to be able to express yourself.*

I'd use my hands.

Does he use his hands, Ms. Wynne?

I don't know.

Stupid, only deaf people do that. Is he deaf?

No.

Is there something wrong with his tongue?

No.

Why doesn't he talk, then?

Why do you think?
Maybe he likes being special.
That's a very interesting idea, Joseph.
Maybe he's afraid.
Afraid to talk? Don't be dumb.
Now, Joseph, that's another interesting idea, too. What are you afraid of, children?
Snakes, Ms. Wynne.
I hate spiders.
I'm not afraid of anything!
Nothing at all, Joseph?
Maybe my big brother. When he's mad.

In school he drew unicorns down the notebook page, next to all his answers. He drew them on his test papers. On the bathroom walls. They needed no signature. Everyone knew he had made them. They were his thumbprints. They were his heartbeats. They were his scars.

Oooooh, he's drawing them things again.
Don't you mess up my *paper, Mr. Philadelphia Carew.*
Leave him alone. He's just a dummy.
Horses don't have horns, dummy.
Here comes Ms. Wynne.
If you children will get back in your seats and stop crowding around Philly. You've all seen him draw unicorns before. Now listen to me, and I mean you, too, Joseph. Fold your hands and lift those shining faces to me. Good. We are going on a field trip this afternoon. Joseph, sit in your seat properly and leave Philly's paper alone. A field trip to Chevril Park. Not now, Joseph, get back in your seat. We will be going after lunch. And *after your spelling test.*

Ooooh, what test, Ms. Wynne?
You didn't say there was going to be a test.

The park was a place of green glades. It had trees shaped like popsicles with the chocolate running down the sides. It had trees like umbrellas that moved mysteriously in the wind. There were hidden ponds and secret streams and moist pathways between, lined with rings of white toadstools and trillium the color of blood. Cooing pigeons walked boldly on the pavement. But in the quiet underbrush hopped little brown birds with white throats. Silent throats.

From far away came a strange, magical song. It sounded like a melody mixed with a gargle, a tune touched by a laugh. It creaked, it hesitated, then it sang again. He had never heard anything like it before.

I hear it, Ms. Wynne. I hear the merry-go-round.
And what does it sound like, children?
It sounds lumpy.
Don't be dumb. It sounds upsy-downsy.
It sounds happy and sad.
Joseph, what do you think it sounds like?
Like another country. Like "The Twilight Zone."

Very good, Joseph. And see, Philly is agreeing with you. And strangely, Joseph, you are right. Merry-go-rounds or carousels are from another country, another world. The first ones were built in France in the late 1700s. The best hand-carved animals still are made in Europe. What kind of animals do you think you'll see on this merry-go-round?

Horses.
Lions.
Tigers.

Camels.
Don't be dumb–camels.
There are too! I been here before. And *elephants.*

He saw unicorns, galloping around and around, a whole herd of them. And now he saw his mistake. They were not like horses or goats or deer or lambs or bulls. They were like–themselves. And with the sun slanting on them from beyond the trees, they were like rainbows, all colors and no colors at all.

Their mouths were open and they were calling. That was the magical song he had heard before. A strange, shimmery kind of cry, not like horses or goats or deer or lambs or bulls; more musical, with a strange rise and fall to each phrase.

He tried to count them as they ran past. Seven, fifteen, twenty-one . . . he couldn't contain them all. Sometimes they doubled back and he was forced to count them again. And again. He settled for the fact that it was a herd of unicorns. No. *Herd* was too ordinary a word for what they were. Horses came in herds. And cows. But unicorns–there had to be a special word for them all together. Suddenly he knew what it was, as if they had told him so in their wavery song. He was watching a *surprise* of unicorns.

Look at old weird Philly. He's just staring at the merry-go-round. Come on, Mr. Philadelphia Chicago New York L.A. Carew. Go on up and ride. They won't bite.

Joseph, keep your mouth shut and you might be able to hear something.

What, Ms. Wynne?

You might hear the heart's music, Joseph. That's a lot more interesting than the flapping of one's own mouth.

What does that mean, Ms. Wynne?

It means shut up, Joseph.

 Ooooh, she got you, Joey.

It means shut up, Denise, too, I bet.

All of you, mouths shut, ears open. We're going for a ride.

We don't have any money, Ms. Wynne.

That's all taken care of. Everyone pick out a horse or a whatever. Mr. Frangipanni, the owner of this carousel, can't wait all day.

Dibs on the red horse.

I got the gray elephant.

Mine's the white horse.

No, Joseph, can't you see Philly has already chosen that one.

But heroes always ride the white horse. And he isn't any kind of hero.

Choose another one, Joseph.

Aaaah, Ms. Wynne, that's not fair.

Why not take the white elephant, Joseph. Hannibal, a great hero of history, marched across the high Alps on elephants to capture Rome.

Wow—did he really?

Really, Joseph.

Okay. Where's Rome?

Who knows where Rome is? I bet Mr. Frangipanni does.

Then ask Mr. Frangipanni!

Italy, Ms. Wynne.

Italy is right. Time to mount up. That's it. We're all ready, Mr. Frangipanni.

The white flank scarcely trembled, but he saw it. "Do not be afraid," he thought. "I couldn't ever hurt you." He placed his hand gently on the tremor and it stopped.

Moving up along the length of the velvety beast, he saw the arched neck ahead of him, its blue veins like tiny rivers branching under the angel-hair mane.

One swift leap and he was on its back. The unicorn turned its head to stare at him with its amber eyes. The horn almost touched his knee. He flinched, pulling his knee up close to his chest. The unicorn turned its head back and looked into the distance.

He could feel it move beneath him, the muscles bunching and flattening as it walked. Then with that strange wild cry, the unicorn leaped forward and began to gallop around and around the glade.

He could sense others near him, catching movement out of the corners of his eyes. Leaning down, he clung to the unicorn's mane. They ran through day and into the middle of night till the stars fell like snow behind them. He heard a great singing in his head and heart and he suddenly felt as if the strength of old kings were running in his blood. He threw his head back and laughed aloud.

Boy, am I dizzy.
My elephant was the best.
I had a red pony. Wow, did we fly!
Everyone dismounted? Now, tell me how you felt.

He slid off the silken side, feeling the solid earth beneath his feet. There was a buzz of voices around him, but he ignored them all. Instead, he turned back to the unicorn and walked toward its head. Standing still, he reached up and brought its horn down until the point rested on his chest. The golden whorls were hard and cold beneath his fingers. And if his fingers seemed to tremble ever so slightly, it was no more than how the unicorn's flesh had shuddered once under the fragile shield of its skin.

He stared into the unicorn's eyes, eyes of antique gold so old, he wondered if they had first looked on the garden where the original thrush had sung the first notes from a hand-painted bush.

Taking his right hand off the horn, he sketched a unicorn in the air between them.

As if that were all the permission it needed, the unicorn nodded its head. The horn ripped his light shirt, right over the heart. He put his left palm over the rip. The right he held out to the unicorn. It nuzzled his hand and its breath was moist and warm.

Look, look at Philly's shirt.

Ooooh, there's blood.

Let me through, children. Thank you, Joseph, for helping him get down. Are you hurt, Philly? Now don't be afraid. Let me see. I could never hurt you. Why, I think there's a cut there. Mr. Frangipanni, come quick. Have you any bandages? The boy is hurt. It's a tiny wound but there's lots of blood so it may be very deep. Does it hurt, dear?

No.

Brave boy. Now be still till Mr. Frangipanni comes.

He spoke, Ms. Wynne. Philly spoke.

Joseph, do be still, I have enough trouble without you . . .

But he spoke, Ms. Wynne. He said "no."

Don't be silly, Joseph.

But he did. He spoke. Didn't you, Philly?

Yes.

Yes.

He turned and looked.

The unicorn nodded its head once and spoke in that high, wavering magical voice. "THE HORN HEALS."

He repeated it.

Yes. The horn heals.

He spoke! He spoke!

I'll just clean this wound, Philly, don't move. Why–that's strange. There's some blood, but only an old scar. Are you sure you're all right, dear?

Yes.

Yes.

As he watched, the unicorn dipped its horn to him once, then whirled away, disappearing into the dappled light of the trees. He wondered if he would ever capture it right on paper. It was nothing like the sketches he had drawn before. Nothing. But he would try.

Yes, Ms. Wynne, an old scar healed. I'm sure.

Jane Yolen

Jane Yolen was born in 1939 in New York City. She holds a M.Ed. from the University of Massachusetts and a Doctor of Law from College of Our Lady of the Elms. Formerly an editor, she has been a full-time professional writer since 1965. Her book The Emperor and the Kite *was an American Library Association Notable Book and Caldecott Honor Book. She has also received the Lewis Carroll Shelf Award, Golden Kite Award, the Christopher Award, and the Caldecott Medal for her picture book* Owl Moon. *Jane Yolen's picture books, novels, and short stories reflect her desire to work fables and folklore motifs into contemporary stories. She has three children and lives in Hatfield, Massachusetts,* USA.

NONE OF MY BUSINESS

Anatoly Aleksin

THE SCHOOL I GO to is the same my mother and father once went to. Nobody remembers my father but a lot of people remember my mother. Our literature teacher who also heads our drama circle said about Mother: "She had highly commendable looks," and gave me an appraising glance. That could be put up with. After all, no one has been given any marks for "commendable looks" as yet. But evidently, as compared to me, mother had a lot of other commendable qualities. For example, there was no record of her ever kicking empty tins with old hockey sticks about the schoolyard, or playing leap-frog.

I didn't know any other details of mother's past, but then one day my grandmother, while helping mother with some household chores, said: "You know Sergei has won a prize in the music competition of our republic."

"Sergei who?" I asked.

"Sergei Potapov. Every cultured person knows him."

"Never heard of him. Who is he?" I said.

And at that moment I caught father's look of love, or rather, gratitude. A momentary look, but it was unmistakable, not that I understood what it was all about.

Later, in the kitchen, Grandmother explained to me that Sergei Potapov used to go to the special school for musically gifted children and that my mother fell in love with him when she was in the fifth class at school.

That music school was, and still is, located right opposite our school, just across the road. When a pupil comes out of our school it is difficult to decide outright whether he is gifted or not. But when he comes out of the doors of that school across the road it is at once clear that he is gifted.

We emerge from school with satchels; the musically gifted ones, with cases. Sergei Potapov first attracted mother's attention because he carried a particularly large case. He played the cello. Then later, in her fifth year at school, she fell in love with him. Mother must have also been a gifted child in her own way. Take me, for example, I'm in the sixth class already and have never yet once fallen in love with anybody.

"Yes, Sergei has certainly made a name for himself," Grandmother said at supper.

Father took a cigarette and began smoking right there in the dining room, though usually he went out to the corridor or to the kitchen to smoke.

"What's the matter?" Mother said. "Oh dear! It was ages ago. Just childish nonsense!" Mother was in high spirits and laughed cheerfully. But father didn't smile once that evening.

"Yes, quite a name, quite . . ." Grandmother kept repeating as she cleared the table.

Grandmother liked to educate us. And she had her own way of doing it.

"My neighbor's son has learned to cook soup," she would say, and I was supposed to understand that it was desirable that I also should learn to cook soup.

"Nikolai, who graduated from the medical college the same year as you, is now the head of a department," she would inform Father, and Father was supposed to draw the conclusion that it would not hurt him to become the head of a department too. The information that "Sergei has made a name for himself" was to imply that it was high time Father did the same.

Two years ago I had to have my tonsils removed. "A trifling operation," everyone said. But I had a different opinion about it. The surgeon who cut them out seemed a wonderful person to me. He caused me awful pain and it would have been only natural for me to hate him, but instead I was fascinated by him–a mixed feeling of fear and admiration. It was hard to imagine that he would take off his white smock and his rubber gloves and turn into an ordinary human being like everybody else. That he might even go to a snack-bar . . .

Father operated every day. And so every day someone looked at him in just the same way as I looked at that surgeon of mine.

"Have you ever had an operation?" I asked Grandmother.

It turned out that in all her sixty years she had never once been operated on. So how could she judge father's worth!

"It's wonderful what people like Sergei Potapov achieve in life," Grandmother still pursued the subject while putting on her overcoat.

"Next time you have your sick headache don't call a doctor, call that cellist of yours," I said. "Let him cure you."

That night when I was cleaning my teeth in the bathroom before going to bed, I overheard Mother say to Father:

"But it's ridiculous!" She was still in that exalted mood. "Honestly, you can't be serious about it. Why, I was twelve years old at the time–in the fifth class."

"It *started* when you were in the fifth class," Father said quietly, and I heard his hand fumbling for the cigarettes in his pocket. A shudder ran through me, as they say in the novels.

So it only started in the fifth class? And when did it end, I should like to know? If it was over in the sixth it can be ignored, but what if it went on till the seventh, or even the ninth?

"Father was in the same class as Mother," I reasoned to myself, "and the school for the gifted ones was right across the road, as it still is; and so their romance went on right under Father's nose. I can imagine what he suffered and what he is still suffering."

Something had to be done about it, but what? Who could advise me? For example, if I asked Grandmother, she would say, "My neighbor's son minds his own business and never interferes in the affairs of the grown-ups."

And maybe it really was none of my business? Maybe indeed . . .

A few days later, before leaving for school, I chanced to hear the TV program for the day, and among other things they mentioned that Sergei Potapov was to play that evening. Fortunately, I was the only one who heard the announcement.

That evening, a few minutes before the concert by the winners of the music competition was due to begin, I settled down to do my homework in the room where we had our TV set.

"We have a test tomorrow," I announced. And so everybody hardly dared to breathe the rest of the evening.

A week later I discovered that a cello performance by Sergei Potapov was to be broadcast over the radio, so a few minutes before the event I spread my books on the kitchen table–our radio is in the kitchen.

"Another test tomorrow," I said, and the radio was kept silent all evening. But Sergei Potapov stubbornly haunted our family.

Once, returning home after the cinema, I saw a poster on a billboard right where Mother and Father caught their tram every morning. The poster had a big portrait of Sergei Potapov on it. My first idea was to tear off the poster and destroy it. I walked past several times, considering the situation and building up my courage . . . In the end I failed to carry out that plan.

When I came home I set out to convince my parents that it was much more convenient to travel by trolleybus than by tram.

"But the trolleybus stop is much farther away," Father argued.

Oh, if he only knew!

"I'll take you there through the neighboring courtyards and you'll see how near it is. No distance at all."

"It is dark and dangerous to go through courtyards," Grandmother intervened as if she deliberately wished to bring Mother face to face with her past.

In the morning I took Mother and Father to the trolleybus stop through the neighboring yards.

"You see what a convenient way it is? And so near!" I rubbed it in. "Besides you use a much more modern means of transport. Not the same as the Metro, but at least not such an old-fashioned conveyance as tram. And, besides, we can all go together almost the whole way to my school."

"Yes, we see so little of you that that alone makes it worth while," Mother agreed. "Why didn't you show us this way before?"

As a matter of fact I was not at all pleased to have my parents seeing me, a sixth class pupil, off to school every morning right in front of my schoolmates. But that was of secondary importance now. And so I succeeded in leading them away from that billboard with the portrait.

Of course, Mother might have chanced to see the poster in some other part of the city, but that was beyond my power to prevent. I could only hope for the best.

A few days later I said:

"We had to write a composition today entitled 'What I Want to Be.' And can you imagine? Almost all the boys wrote that they wanted to be doctors. Almost all of them. Not fliers, or divers, or cellists, but physicians, doctors. And the teacher said that there was nothing surprising about it. The most noble profession in the world!

 They want to help people, to cure them, to save their lives. A natural desire!"

"Yes, of course," Mother said.

But Father and Grandmother kept silent.

One Sunday I brought home with me my pal, Vasili Paganini. Paganini is a nickname, of course. Vasili plays the violin and goes to the music school for gifted children.

"Do you like Sergei Prokofiev?" I asked Vasili, choosing a moment when all the family was gathered together.

"Of course," Vasili answered.

"And Sergei Rachmaninov?"

"Naturally. Who doesn't love his music?"

"And Sergei Potapov?"

"Never heard of him."

"Never once? Think hard. Try to remember."

"No, never heard of him. And why should you be interested in this . . . what's his name? Why on earth?" Vasili asked with genuine amazement, as if we hadn't rehearsed the whole scene fifteen minutes ago in our bathroom.

"Well now, if even Paganini knows nothing of his existence!" I exclaimed looking at all the members of our family in turn.

And yet my mother's past refused to be crossed out and be done away with.

One morning, at one and the same time, two postcards came from my school. In general I don't like when my parents get postcards from school. So this time, sort of by chance, I glanced at them more closely. As it happened they had nothing to do with my person. They were invitations to Mother and Father to a traditional "joint" gathering of former pupils of the two schools, ours and the music school. The invitations were sent a whole week in advance with a request to inform all their former classmates whose whereabouts they might chance to know.

I immediately thought that Sergei Potapov was sure to be present at that gathering. "They organize these get-togethers as a pleasant treat for former pupils," I reasoned, "but what pleasure would my father get watching Mother in the grip of all sorts of reminiscences? And those reminiscences were sure to crowd in on her, even if only for a few minutes . . . And then father would start smoking, forgetting to go out into the corridor . . ."

I took the postcards and tucked them into my satchel.

The first thing I saw in our school entrance hall was a huge poster advertising the coming traditional joint gathering of former pupils. At the bottom was the announcement in black letters on white: "Our concert program will include a cello performance by Sergei Potapov, prize winner in the music competition of our republic."

Aha, I thought, so there he would be demonstrating his achievements in front of everybody! And they would all applaud him. But Father wouldn't be able to demonstrate *his* achievements in public. He couldn't cut out somebody's appendix right there on the stage. Yes, Sergei Potapov would definitely win the day.

The day after the traditional gathering, our literature teacher who so well remembered my mother's "commendable looks" asked me:

"Why didn't your mother come?"

She asked it just as if I had no father at all. I spread out my hands in a gesture of complete bewilderment. I mastered that trick a long time ago. When you don't want to lie and don't want to say either "yes" or "no," you just spread your hands in innocent bewilderment. And let those who've asked the question make whatever they like of it.

That same day when mother came home from work she quickly entered the room without even taking off her coat, a sign that boded no good.

"Wasn't there any message for me and Father from the school?" she asked.

I used my well-tried trick of spreading my hands, but it didn't work.

"Didn't they send anything for us?" she repeated.

"Yes, they did send something."

"What do you mean 'something'? Don't you remember exactly what it was?"

"Yes, I remember. They sent you two postcards. I tucked them into my satchel quite absentmindedly . . . We had a test that day and I forgot."

"Do you have a test every day now?"

"No, not every day, but fairly often. Here are the postcards!"

I handed them to her but she never even looked at them. She wouldn't take her eyes off me.

"What on earth have you done to be so afraid of our coming to the school?"

"I haven't done anything. And I wasn't afraid. I just forgot, that's all."

"But they say there was an announcement put up at school?"

"I just didn't notice it."

"You forgot, you just didn't notice . . . That's awful. It shows your complete indifference. It's dreadful! Don't you understand what a pleasure it would have been for me to meet my old friends? Friends whom I haven't seen for so many years?"

And Mother sank heavily into an armchair, still in her coat, without even unbuttoning it.

"All right, you never thought of letting me enjoy myself, but what about Father? Doesn't his happiness mean anything to you either?"

What could I say to that?

Fortunately, at that moment grandmother entered the room

and declared: "By the way, my neighbor's son has again received top marks at school and, besides, he has learned to cook jellied fruit."

Translated by Valentina Jacque

Anatoly Aleksin

Anatoly Aleksin was born in 1924 in Moscow. As a dramatist and author of books for both children and young adults, he has won many prizes for his writing, including the Lenin Komsomol Prize, the Hans Christian Andersen International Diploma, and a Mildred Batchelder Award nomination for his book A Late Born Child. *Mr. Aleksin has authored over one hundred books, amongst them:* My Brother Plays the Clarinet, The Third in the Fifth Row, Crazy Yevdokia, Just Ring Up and Come, Signalmen and Trumpeters. *His work has been translated into forty-four languages around the world.*

THE STORY OF THE BLUE BEACH

Scott O'Dell

MY FATHER WORE the heaviest of his leather breeches, his thickest jacket, and a pair of high horsehide boots. It was gear for the wild country that lay between the Ranch of the Two Brothers and Blue Beach. He carried his best musket, his tinderbox, and his powder horn. I dressed accordingly, but carried no weapon except a knife.

There were four horses saddled and waiting for us. I rode my stallion, Tiburón, and I rode astride.

The river would still be running a torrent. It was much easier to cross close to the ranch and go down the south bank, but we had no desire to get soaked so early on the journey.

Accordingly, we chose the north bank and followed it through heavy chaparral and patches of cactus until we had ridden for two hours.

Where the river widened and ran knee-deep, we crossed to the south bank. It was still a good hour's ride from the Blue Beach. But it was here that we took the first precaution.

My father and I had been coming to Blue Beach for two years. On the three journeys we had made, we had always been followed. Sometimes by one or two Indians, sometimes by more. But to this day, no one had followed us farther than this west crossing. Here we had managed to elude them.

One thing that helped was that we never told anyone our secret—the story of the Blue Beach.

We told none of the vaqueros or the *mayordomo*. Nor Rosario, though Rosario could be trusted. Nor my sister, who could not be. Nor even Doña Dolores, whom we could trust most of all. Dolores you could hang by her thumbs and still not hear one word that she did not wish to speak.

There was no way to find the Blue Beach except by following the river, either down from the mountains or up from the sea. From the sea no one would ever find it because of a series of lagoons. From the direction of the mountains you would need to be very lucky, as lucky as we had been in the beginning.

The river at this point, where it fanned out into the deep lagoons, ran narrow, between two sheer walls of granite, where even a mountain goat would be lost. At the bottom of these cliffs were two beaches, one facing the other across a distance of a hundred steps.

The beaches were strips of fine sand, finer than the sand you find on the sea beach itself. Both had a bluish cast, like pebbles you see through clear, running water. But they also had another color, a lighter blue that had a look of metal, as if there were copper deposits in the cliffs that had been washed down by the river and the rain and had mixed with the lighter color.

Someone might call the beaches green or the color of turquoise, but to us they were blue and this is what we called them–the Blue Beaches, more often, the Blue Beach.

On this day, as on the three other journeys we had made to the Blue Beach, we tied our horses and climbed up from the stream to a towering rock. This was where we took our second precaution, for from this high place we could survey the trails, one coming along the river, and one from the sea.

"What do you see?" my father said. He liked to test my eyesight. "Are we followed?"

"I see nothing on the trail," I said, "either from the river or from the sea."

"What is the brown spot among the oaks?"
"Where?"
"Up the river about a hundred *varas.*"
"I see nothing."
"Look once more."
"Does it move?"
"Judge for yourself. But first you need to find it."
I looked hard and at last made out the brown spot among the oaks. "It is a cow grazing," I said.
"There are two, and one is not a cow but a yearling fawn. What do you hear?"
"The stream."
"What else?"
"A crow somewhere."
"Is that all?"
"Yes."
"Listen."
"A woodpecker behind us."
"Yes. And what else do you hear?"
"Nothing."
"Besides the stream and the surf at the mouth of the river and gulls fishing?"
"You have good ears."
"And you will have them someday."
"Never so good as yours."
"Better. *Mucho más.*"
Don Saturnino was silent for a while. Then he said, "Tomorrow is Carlos's birthday. He would have been eighteen had he lived."
"He would have liked these journeys," I answered.
"Perhaps. Perhaps not. Who knows? It is sufficient that you like them. You do like them, Carlota?"
"Everything, Father," I said. "Everything."

Here we sat for an hour, to make sure that we had not been followed.

When the sun was overhead, we crawled down from the pinnacle. We reached the Blue Beach and took off our boots and stepped out into the middle of the stream. We made our way for a distance of some fifty paces, leaving no tracks behind us. A clump of willows grew amidst a pile of driftwood and boulders at this place. Here the river divided and ran in two smaller streams on both sides of the willows.

The boulders could not be seen at high tide. But the tide was low now and they stuck up in two crescents, facing each other and leaving a clear space between them. The water was cold, both the sea water that met the river at this point, and likewise the river water itself.

Stripped to my singlet, I splashed water on my legs, on my arms and chest. I had found that the best way to approach cold water was by small shivers, suffered one at a time.

Throwing out my arms, I took in a great gulp of air, held it for a minute, counting each second. Then I let out all the air in a quick whoosh. Then I raised my arms again and took in a greater gulp.

This air I held for two minutes, still counting the seconds in my mind–one second, two seconds, and so forth. I repeated this three times. The third time I counted up to four minutes.

It had taken me two years to build up to where I could hold my breath for this length of time. My father had heard of pearl divers in La Paz who could hold their breath for five minutes and even longer. I had tried this but had fainted.

Carefully we stepped into the wide pool between the two crescents of stone, beneath the canopy of willows. We inched our way to the center of the pool, cautious not to rile the sand.

As my foot touched a smooth slab of stone, I stooped down, lifted it with much care, and set it to one side. Beneath it was a rock-lined hole filled with water, the size of my body and twice its height.

At the bottom of this hole was something that, when we first saw it, seemed to be the trunk of a tree–a tree washed down from the mountains. Undoubtedly, it once had risen above the water, but over the years floods had worn it away to a worm-eaten stump.

It had been the mainmast of a ship, which my father said was some seventy feet in length. It had the wide beam, the high stern, of the galleons that two centuries before had sailed the seas between China and the coast of California and Mexico.

These ships, my father said, came on favorable winds and currents to northern California, then along the coast south to the ports of San Blas and Acapulco. They carried great treasures from the Indies, these galleons, so great that they became the prey of American and English pirates.

Some of these treasure ships had been captured. On some, their crews had died of scurvy. Others had run aground through careless navigation. Others were driven ashore by storms. Still others had sought refuge from their pursuers by hiding in lagoons such as the one at Blue Beach.

"This must have been a large lagoon at one time," my father said when we first discovered the galleon. "A good place to hide a ship. But when it was once inside, something happened to the ship and it never returned to the sea."

Hidden in the galleon's hold, near the stump of the mainmast, were two chests filled with coins. The coins were of pure gold. They showed three castles and the two flying doves that meant they had been struck in the mint at Lima, Peru. The date marked upon each coin that we carried away on the trips we had made was the year of Our Lord 1612.

The two chests–each made of hard wood banded with iron straps and sealed with a hasp that had rusted and fallen off–were well beneath the surface of the water, whether at low tide or in the summer, when the stream ran low. This was fortunate, for had the chests been exposed, some passing Indian or vaquero would have discovered them.

There were many things to do before the chests could be reached. Usually it took me half a day to bring up a pouch of coins from the sunken ship.

The place where I dove, which was surrounded by jagged rocks and driftwood, was too narrow for my father. He had tried to squeeze through when we first discovered the galleon, but partway down he got stuck and I had to pull him back. It was my task, therefore, to go into the cavelike hole. My father stood beside it and helped me to go down and to come up.

I buckled a strong belt around my waist and to it tied a riata that was ten *varas* long and stout enough to hold a stallion. I fastened my knife to my wrist—a two-edged blade made especially for me by our blacksmith—to protect myself against spiny rays and the big eels that could sting you to death. In the many dives I had made, I never had seen a shark.

Taking three deep breaths, I prepared to let myself down into the hole. In one hand I held a sink-stone, heavy enough to weigh me down. I let out all the air in my chest, took a deep breath, and held it. Then I began the descent.

The sink-stone would have taken me down fast, but the edges of the rocky hole were sharp. I let myself down carefully, one hand-hold at a time. It took me about a minute to reach the rotted deck where the chests lay. I now had two minutes to pry the coins loose and carry them to the surface. We had tried putting the coins in a leather sack and hoisting them to the surface. But we had trouble with this because of the currents that swept around the wreck.

The coins lay in a mass, stuck together, lapping over each other and solid as rock. They looked, when I first saw them, like something left on the stove too long. I always expected to find them gone, but now as I walked toward the chests, with the stone holding me down, I saw that they were still there. No one had come upon them during the seven months since our last visit.

The first time I had dived and brought up a handful of coins, I said to my father that we should empty both the chests and take the coins home.

"Then everyone would talk," Don Saturnino said. "As soon as they saw the gold coins the news would spread the length of California."

"We don't need to tell anyone. I can hide them in my chest at home."

"The news would fly out before the sun set. At the ranch there are many eyes."

I still thought it was a better idea to empty the chests before someone else did, but I could see that my father enjoyed these days, when the two of us went to the Blue Beach, so I said no more.

The sun was overhead and its rays slanted down through the narrow crevice. There were many pieces of debris on the deck and I had to step carefully. With my knife I pried loose a handful of coins. They were of a dark green color and speckled here and there with small barnacles. I set the coins aside.

My lungs were beginning to hurt, but I had not felt the tug of the riata yet, the signal from my father that I had been down three minutes. I pried loose a second handful and put my knife away. Before the tug came I dropped my sink-stone and took up the coins. Gold is very heavy, much heavier than stones of the same size.

Fish were swimming around me as I went up through the hole of rocks and tree trunks, but I saw no stingrays or eels. I did see a shark lying back on a ledge, but he was small and gray, a sand shark, which is not dangerous.

On my third trip down, I hauled up about the same number of coins as the other times. The pouch we had brought was now full. I asked my father if we had enough.

"Are you tired?" he said.

"Yes, a little."

"Can you go down again?"

"Yes."

I dived twice more. It was on the last dive that I had the trouble. The tug on the riata had not come, but I was tired, so I started away from the chest with one handful of coins. Close to the chests, between them and the hole, I had noticed what seemed to be two pieces of timber covered with barnacles. They looked as if they might be part of a third and larger chest.

I still held my knife and I thrust it at a place where the two gray timbers seemed to join. It was possible that I had found another chest filled with coins.

As the knife touched them, the two timbers moved a little. Instantly, I felt pressure upon my wrist. I drew back the hand that held the knife. Rather, I tried to draw it back, but it would not move. The tide had shifted the timbers somehow and I was caught. So I thought.

I felt a tug upon the riata fastened to my waist. It was the signal from my father to come to the surface. I answered him with two quick tugs of the leather rope.

Now I felt a hot pain run up my arm. I tried to open my fingers, to drop the knife, but my hand was numb. Then as I stared down into the murky water I saw a slight movement where my hand was caught. At the same moment I saw a flash of pink, a long fleshy tongue sliding along my wrist.

I had never seen a burro clam, but I had heard the tales about them, for there were many on our coast. Attached to rocks or timbers, they grew to half the height of a man, these gray, silent monsters. Many unwary fishermen had lost their lives in the burrows' jaws.

The pain in my arm was not so great now as the hot pains in my chest. I gave a long, hard tug on the riata to let my father know that I was in trouble. Again I saw a flash of pink as the burro opened its lips a little, and the fat tongue slid back and forth.

I dropped the coins I held in my other hand. The burro had closed once more on my wrist. But shortly it began to open again, and I felt a sucking pressure, as if the jaws were trying to draw me inside the giant maw.

Putting my knees against the rough bulge of the shell, as the jaws opened and then began to close, I jerked with all my strength. I fell slowly backward upon the ship's deck. My hand was free. With what breath I had I moved toward the hole. I saw the sun shining above and climbed toward it. The next thing I saw was my father's face and I was lying on the river's sandy bank. He took my knife in his hand.

After I told him what had happened, my father said, "The knife saved your life. The burro clamped down upon it. See the mark here. The steel blade kept its jaws open. Enough to let you wrench yourself free."

He pulled me to my feet and I put on my leather pants and coat.

"Here," he said, passing the reins of his bay gelding to me, "ride Santana. He goes gentler than Tiburón."

"I'll ride my own horse," I said.

"Good, if you wish it."

"I wish it," I said, knowing that he didn't want me to say that my hand was numb.

"Does the hand hurt?"

"No."

"Some?"

"No."

"You were very brave," he said.

My father wanted me to be braver than I was. I wanted to say I was scared, both when the burro had hold of me and now, at this moment, but I didn't because he expected me to be as brave as Carlos. It was at times like this that I was angry at my father and at my dead brother, too.

"It was good fortune," I said.

"Fortune and bravery often go together," Don Saturnino said.

Scott O'Dell

Scott O'Dell was born in 1903 in Los Angeles. He attended Stanford University and the University of Rome. Formerly a cameraman and book editor for a major newspaper, he has been a full-time writer since 1934. His many prestigious awards include Newbery Medals, the Hans Christian Andersen Medal, the German Juvenile International Award, and the Regina Medal. His most famous book, Island of the Blue Dolphins, *has won many awards, and is considered an American classic. That book and his* The Black Pearl *were made into movies. He lives with his wife on Make Peace Hill in Waccabuc, New York,* USA.

THE PEOPLE COULD FLY

Virginia Hamilton

THEY SAY THE people could fly. Say that long ago in Africa, some of the people knew magic. And they would walk up on the air like climbin' up on a gate. And they flew like blackbirds over the fields. Black, shiny wings flappin' against the blue up there.

Then, many of the people were captured for slavery. The ones that could fly shed their wings. They couldn't take their wings across the water on the slave ships. Too crowded, don't you know.

The folks were full of misery, then. Got sick with the up and down of the sea. So they forgot about flyin' when they could no longer breathe the sweet scent of Africa.

Say the people who could fly kept their power, although they shed their wings. They kept their secret magic in the land of slavery. They looked the same as the other people from Africa who had been coming over, who had dark skin. Say you couldn't tell anymore one who could fly from one who couldn't.

One such who could was an old man, call him Toby. And standin' tall, yet afraid, was a young woman who once had wings. Call her Sarah. Now Sarah carried a babe tied to her back. She trembled to be so hard worked and scorned.

The slaves labored in the fields from sunup to sundown. The owner of the slaves callin' himself their Master. Say he was a hard lump of clay. A hard, glinty coal. A hard rock pile, wouldn't be moved. His Overseer on horseback pointed out the slaves who were slowin' down. So the one called Driver cracked his whip over the slow ones to make them move faster. That whip was a slice-open cut of pain. So they did move faster. Had to.

Sarah hoed and chopped the row as the babe on her back slept.

Say the child grew hungry. That babe started up bawlin' too loud. Sarah couldn't stop to feed it. Couldn't stop to soothe and quiet it down. She let it cry. She didn't want to. She had no heart to croon to it.

"Keep that thing quiet," called the Overseer. He pointed his finger at the babe. The woman scrunched low. The Driver cracked his whip across the babe anyhow. The babe hollered like any hurt child, and the woman fell to the earth.

The old man that was there, Toby, came and helped her to her feet.

"I must go soon," she told him.

"Soon," he said.

Sarah couldn't stand up straight any longer. She was too weak. The sun burned her face. The babe cried and cried, "Pity me, oh, pity me," say it sounded like. Sarah was so sad and starvin', she sat down in the row.

"Get up, you black cow," called the Overseer. He pointed his hand, and the Driver's whip snarled around Sarah's legs. Her sack dress tore into rags. Her legs bled onto the earth. She couldn't get up.

Toby was there where there was no one to help her and the babe.

"Now, before it's too late," panted Sarah. "Now, Father!"

"Yes, Daughter, the time is come," Toby answered. "Go, as you know how to go!"

He raised his arms, holding them out to her. *"Kum . . . yali, kum buba tambe,"* and more magic words, said so quickly, they sounded like whispers and sighs.

The young woman lifted one foot on the air. Then the other. She flew clumsily at first, with the child now held tightly in her arms.

Then she felt the magic, the African mystery. Say she rose just as free as a bird. As light as a feather.

The Overseer rode after her, hollerin'. Sarah flew over the fences. She flew over the woods. Tall trees could not snag her. Nor could the Overseer. She flew like an eagle now, until she was gone from sight. No one dared speak about it. Couldn't believe it. But it was, because they that was there saw that it was.

Say the next day was dead hot in the fields. A young man slave fell from the heat. The Driver come and whipped him. Toby come over and spoke words to the fallen one. The words of ancient Africa once heard are never remembered completely. The young man forgot them as soon as he heard them. They went way inside him. He got up and rolled over on the air. He rode it awhile. And he flew away.

Another and another fell from the heat. Toby was there. He cried out to the fallen and reached his arms out to them. *"Kum kunka yali, kum . . . tambe!"* Whispers and sighs. And they too rose on the air. They rode the hot breezes. The ones flyin' were black and shinin' sticks, wheelin' above the head of the Overseer. They crossed the rows, the fields, the fences, the streams, and were away.

"Seize the old man!" cried the Overseer. "I heard him say the magic *words.* Seize him!"

The one callin' himself Master come runnin'. The Driver got his whip ready to curl around old Toby and tie him up. The slave owner took his hip gun from its place. He meant to kill old, black Toby.

But Toby just laughed. Say he threw back his head and said, "Hee, hee! Don't you know who I am? Don't you know some of us in this field?" He said it to their faces. "We are ones who fly!"

And he sighed the ancient words that were a dark promise. He said them all around to the others in the field under the whip, *". . . buba yali . . . buba tambe . . ."*

There was a great outcryin'. The bent backs straighted up. Old and young who were called slaves and could fly joined hands. Say like they would ring-sing. But they didn't shuffle in a circle. They didn't sing. They rose on the air. They flew in a flock that was black against the heavenly blue. Black crows or black shadows. It didn't matter, they went so high. Way above the plantation, way over the slavery land. Say they flew away to *Free-dom.*

And the old man, old Toby, flew behind them, takin' care of them. He wasn't cryin'. He wasn't laughin'. He was the seer. His gaze fell on the plantation where the slaves who could not fly waited.

"Take us with you!" Their looks spoke it but they were afraid to shout it. Toby couldn't take them with him. Hadn't the time to teach them to fly. They must wait for a chance to run.

"Goodie-bye!" The old man called Toby spoke to them, poor souls! And he was flyin' gone.

So they say. The Overseer told it. The one called Master said it was a lie, a trick of the light. The Driver kept his mouth shut.

The slaves who could not fly told about the people who could fly to their children. When they were free. When they sat close before the fire in the free land, they told it. They did so love firelight and *Free-dom,* and tellin'.

They say that the children of the ones who could not fly told their children. And now, me, I have told it to you.

The People Could Fly is one of the most extraordinary, moving tales in black folklore. It almost makes us believe that the people *could* fly. There are numerous separate accounts of flying Africans and slaves in the black folktale literature. Such accounts are often combined with tales of slaves disappearing. A plausible explanation might be the slaves running away from slavery, slipping away while in the fields or under cover of darkness. In code language murmured from one slave to another, "Come fly away!" might have been the words used. Another explanation is the wish-fulfillment motif.

The magic hoe variant is often combined with the flying-African tale. A magic hoe is left still hoeing in an empty field after all the slaves have flown away. Magic with the hoe and other farm tools, and the power of disappearing are often attributed to Gullah (Angolan) African slaves. Angolan slaves were thought by other slaves to have exceptional powers.

The People Could Fly is a detailed fantasy tale of suffering, of magic power exerted against the so-called Master and his underlings. Finally, it is a powerful testament to the millions of slaves who never had the opportunity to "fly" away. They remained slaves, as did their children. *The People Could Fly* was first told and retold by those who had only their imaginations to set them free.

Virginia Hamilton

Virginia Hamilton, born in 1936 in Yellow Springs, Ohio, is one of the most distinguished and influential authors of fiction for children today. M.C. Higgins the Great *was awarded more honors the year it was published than any other children's book. Ms. Hamilton has received the Newbery Medal, the Boston Globe-Horn Book Award, the National Book Award, the Coretta Scott King Award and the Edgar Allan Poe Award for the best juvenile mystery for* The House of Dies Drear. *Virginia Hamilton was educated at Antioch College and Ohio State University and did further study in literature and the novel at the New School for Social Research.* The People Could Fly *draws upon her lifetime interest in and study of folklore. She is married to the poet Arnold Adoff; they have two children and live in Yellow Springs, Ohio,* USA.

EDŽIŅŠ

Vilis Lacis

THE HIGHWAY turned up onto a small hill, and Edžiņš stopped for a moment to have a look around. The eastern horizon shone with the golden rays of the sun, but the forests and valleys still lay in deep shadow. Roosters crowed in peasants' farmyards, and somewhere a scythe rang out, but no early morning reaper was to be seen.

The highway was hazy with dust. As far as the eye could see, there were people, alone and in groups, traveling light, carrying only small bundles on their backs. They were all heading north-west, in the same direction that caravans of carts and columns of trucks had been moving all night.

Edžiņš and his mother had also been walking all night. When they had been fired upon twice from the forest, they had clambered down into the roadside ditch, and, crouching for as long as the firing continued, proceeded on their way. Edžiņš could have walked at a much faster pace, but then his mother could not have kept up. They took turns carrying their small bundle, which consisted of a blanket, a towel, and some food.

Only with daybreak did Edžiņš see how his mother's face had turned grey from road dust. He himself could feel the grit in his teeth.

"Mama . . . Let's take a break down by the river to wash and have something to eat."

"All right, Edžiņš," his mother answered. It was not clear whether

her voice was weak from fatigue or from deep sorrow. She brushed her rough, toil-worn hand over her son's forehead, and cast a mournful glance at the boy's figure.

They moved on until they came upon a small river off to the side of the road, where they washed the dust from their faces, necks, and hands. The July sun, which had just begun to peer through the tree tops, immediately started to beat down upon them. They sat down in the shadow of some bushes, and Edžiņš's mother unbound the bundle with the food, revealing half a round loaf of rye bread and four hard-boiled eggs.

"Edžiņš, have something to eat," she said. She herself broke off a small piece of bread and, crumb by crumb, put it into her mouth, chewing long and slow, as if she had no desire to eat. Seeing this, Edžiņš peeled two eggs and shoved one into his mother's hand.

"Mama, eat. You didn't eat anything all day yesterday."

"I don't feel like it."

"No, you have to eat, otherwise you won't have the strength to walk."

Edžiņš knew that his mother was saving the food for him. He was starving, as boys his age always are, but out of shame he could not touch the bread while his mother refused to eat. This continued until his mother relented and took a bite from her egg. Edžiņš chewed his piece of bread, looked at the river current and thought: Maybe this is the Aiviekste. In that case this water runs on to merge with the Daugava, and from there it flows on past our house straight to the sea. How long will it take this water to get to Karklaji? He clearly pictured his family's little house on the banks of the Daugava, where he was born and raised, the small bridge with the boats tied up, the fish nets stretched out on the banks, the huge boulder in the middle of the yard, on which his mother used to scrub the laundry . . . He saw it clearly, as if it was all now before his eyes. His heart grew heavy with these thoughts. He became even more despondent when he remembered his father, a river pilot . . . He had taught Edžiņš how to row a boat properly, and taken him along on fishing trips. He remembered how he had scolded Edžiņš when for the first time the boy swam to the other bank of the Daugava and back again. But now his father was dead. In the first days of the war he had reported to his fighting unit and very soon had been sent to look for German saboteurs who had been dropped by parachute to destroy railroad tracks and telephone lines. He and his comrades destroyed several such detachments, but then he was brought home seriously wounded. All night long blood flowed from his mouth. In the morning he was laid in a makeshift plank coffin and buried in the garden behind the house. Immediately afterwards, Edžiņš and his mother were forced to flee.

Edžiņš put his half-eaten chunk of bread back into the bundle. Enough . . . he did not want any more. He broke off a dry twig from the bush and threw it into the water. The twig slowly drifted away on the current. Maybe the water would carry it to the Daugava, beyond Kegums, to their home. There perhaps it would drift off to the side and come to rest on the bank of the river by the little bridge.

Again and again his thoughts brought him back to his native village, and he dreamt that he was still there. This he desired more than anything.

An unexpected commotion on the highway shook him out of his sleepy daydream. People who had previously been calmly walking along the road suddenly started hurrying, throwing themselves into a run. Alarmed, they shouted to one another, and peered into the sky. Several dived into the road-side ditch, while others made a break for the edge of the forest through the open fields. But the forest was nearly a kilometer away. Several women with children pressed themselves against the walls of a grey wooden building standing off to the side of the road. Two young men on bicycles raced across a bridge, still hoping to make it to the forest.

 Airplanes droned in the sky. Edžiņš saw three Nazi bombers. They flew so low that it was possible to make out the heads of the pilots in their cockpits. One plane flew straight along the highway, barely clearing the telegraph poles, flanked by the other two planes. Edžiņš vividly saw several small black lumps detach themselves from the planes . . . Explosions ripped the air, and columns of earth and dust shot skyward. The small grey building where the women had taken shelter with their children collapsed. Telephone wires snapped, and several telephone poles crashed to the ground. Here and there people started to fall. When the rumble of the planes died away, the groans of the wounded, the weeping of women and children's screams were heard. The destroyed building blazed.

"We've got to get away from the road!" Edžiņš cried to his mother. They quickly tied up their bundle, and turned to make a run for the rye fields, where the people who had started to run earlier were trying to hide. At that moment the roar of engines was heard again–and it was closing in. The Nazi vultures were returning. One plane levelled out straight over the rye field. Machine guns opened fire, and here and there the wounded fell. With monstrous delight the Nazi pilots chased their fleeing victims, who were running singly and in groups. Bombs continued to fall, and machine guns pelted the highway in a relentless hail of bullets.

There was nowhere to run to.

"Mama–get down!"

They threw themselves under the bushes and froze. Edžiņš did not take his eyes off the ferociously screaming planes, while all the time his mother's hand instinctively clutched his shoulder, as if protecting him. One plane banked in the air and bore down straight onto the place where they were hiding. All around bullets whistled. Just as the vulture's shadow passed over the bush, Edžiņš felt his mother's body heavy against him. The hand that had been grasping his shoulder slid downward.

"Edžiņš . . . my son," escaped from his mother's very bosom, like a groan. Then she was silent and her eyes, clouded with tears and dimming quickly, looked into the sky.

"Mama, what's the matter? Are you hurt?" For some unknown reason Edžiņš whispered, although everything around him thundered. His mother did not answer. A blood-red spot grew beneath her blouse. She was dead. Edžiņš carefully laid her head on the grass and sat back next to her, not letting her lifeless hand fall from his.

For half an hour the Nazi pilots raged above the highway and then disappeared.

Those who remained alive crawled out of the roadside ditch, emerged from the rye fields, and continued on their way. Passing Red Army soldiers picked up the wounded. The dead were dragged off the road and covered. A woman who had lost her mind walked among the hot ruins, softly singing to the mutilated child in her arms.

After some time a truck stopped on the road right alongside the place where Edžiņš was sitting. Red Army soldiers invited Edžiņš into the truck, but he merely shook his head and remained sitting. The truck drove on. An uninterrupted but diminishing stream of refugees filed past. Evening encroached, and gave way to a short summer night. All the while Edžiņš sat next to his mother's body, holding her cold hand in his.

Early in the morning on the other side of the road five men appeared. They were moving in the opposite direction of the flow of refugees. Each of the five had hidden under his jacket a dismantled rifle, and hand grenades were tucked into their belts. They noticed the boy at the side of the road. His strange, burning look caught their attention, and they walked up to him.

"What's the matter, boy? What are you doing here?"

Edžiņš nodded towards his mother.

"They shot my mother down . . . from an aeroplane." A lump

formed in Edžiņš's throat, and he began to tremble with rage. He forced back the tears.

"Aren't you Jan Karklajs's son?" asked one of the men. Edžiņš looked up at him and recognized Kalejs, a young workmate of his father's.

"My mother must be buried," Edžiņš said.

"We'll take care of that," Kalejs answered.

On a picturesque little hill, twenty paces from where the murderers' bullets had cut short Edžiņš's mother's life, a grave was dug. Edžiņš brought a huge armful of fragrant grass, and lined the bottom of the pit. When the grave had been filled in, he laid at its head a bouquet of wild field flowers.

From the men's conversation Edžiņš came to understand that all five of them were returning to the banks of the Daugava, in the direction of the enemy, to live in the forests and, weapons in hand, fight the invaders and traitors who had deprived Edžiņš of all that was most precious to him–father, mother, native land, and childhood.

"Take me with you," he pleaded. "I'm already twelve years old. I'll be of good use to you. I'll learn how to shoot and throw grenades. I'll be a scout. I'm not afraid of anything."

The men talked it over, and after Kalejs had told them about Edžiņš's father, they agreed.

Leaving, Edžiņš bade farewell to his mother's grave with a long gaze, committing the place forever to his memory . . . And as long as the fresh, sandy hill was visible from the road, he turned his head to look. The men pretended not to notice.

They were walking back, to the south, to avenge Edžiņš's father and mother, and many boys and girls, all those, in fact, who had been crushed by the murderous boot of the enemy.

Translated by Paul Dieterich

Vilis Lacis

Vilis Lacis (1904–1966) was born in Vecmilgravis, on the outskirts of Riga, to the family of a port worker, and he spent his childhood among fishermen. He was a state and public figure, and honored as a People's Writer of the Latvian SSR and winner of the State Prize of the USSR. He authored many popular novels, scripts, and plays, including: The Fisherman's Son, To the New Shore, *as well as children's books* Blacksmiths of the Future *and* Eaglet.

THE BLACK STONE

Katherine Paterson

HE WISHED he'd worn a cap. His mother was always after him to wear something on his head, which made it hard for him simply to go to the closet, take a cap off the hook, and put it on. Today she was at work and wouldn't have known whether he wore one, but the habit of resisting was too strong. It hadn't occurred to him that in the empty sweep between the Washington Monument and the Lincoln Memorial he would have liked to have something to keep the wind from making his ears ache and throb. The metal frames of his glasses cut icily into both sides of his head.

His eyes hurt, too, from straining to find what he had come to see. It was nowhere. The guy at the Metro had told him it was beyond the Washington Monument, but there was nothing to be seen but a grassy expanse of parkland. There were no park police, hardly any people around at all. And he was shy about asking those few he saw. How stupid not to know where the Vietnam memorial was. The papers had been full of it last fall. Everyone knew where it was, except him.

At last he saw the sign, small and not very high, that pointed in the same direction he was headed. And then, without warning, he was there. A sidewalk led him beside a black stone wall that grew down into the earth, getting taller as he walked slowly toward the lowest point, and then gradually diminishing again as the path went up–like a beautifully polished giant boomerang cutting into the surface of the lawn—and covered with names etched exquisitely into the ebony face of the rock.

There were other people on the walk, standing before panels of the shining stone, searching the infinite lines of names and, finding one, fingering the contours of the letters. Park, too, felt the urge to reach out and feel the surface of the stone, but he clenched his fist in his pocket. The first name he touched must be his father's.

> And when they were all gathered in the great hall at Camelot to celebrate the feast of Pentecost, suddenly the mighty doors were opened and a light shone brighter than seven suns. And there entered into the hall, borne by an unseen arm, the Holy Grail, draped in a cloth of blinding white. Then the hall was filled with the odors of meats and wines and they all ate and were filled from the bounty of the Holy Vessel, and no man knew whence it came nor whither it had departed. The knight sat in silence, bedazzled by the vision, and swelling up in his heart was the command, "Follow. Follow and find."

But how was he to find his father's name? The names went on and on; there were thousands of them. He would never find just one.

"Are you looking for someone special?" He turned to see a middle-aged woman in a beige felt hat and tweed overcoat. "It's all right," she said, smiling. "That's what I'm here for, to help." She led him back to the top of the walk, where there was a line of books like the metropolitan area telephone books. She opened one. "What name were you looking for?" she asked gently.

He cleared his throat. "Parkington Waddell Broughton the Fourth," he said.

She searched the book and then put her gloved finger on a place. "Panel 1 W," she said, "line 119."

He stood there, not certain what she meant. "It's this way," she said with her elegant, gentle smile, and led him down to where the black granite was tallest.

She showed him how to count by the marks at the end of every tenth line and then left him to count down for himself, as though she knew he wouldn't want a stranger with him when he first saw it. And there it was: PARKINGTON W. BROUGHTON IV.

He reached out, grateful that on that tall stone the name he needed could be reached, and lightly traced the letters of his father's name. The stone felt warm from the winter sun. It wasn't like a gravestone at all. It was like something alive and lovely. He could see his own hand reflected across his father's name. Tears started in his eyes, surprising him, because he felt so happy to be here, so close to actually touching that handsome man in his jaunty cap with the tie of his uniform loose and the neck unbuttoned.

He wished he had brought something to leave. Other people had left flowers or a single carnation stuck into the seam of the stone beside a name. There were medals and campaign ribbons at the foot of some of the panels and, further to one end, a teddy bear, propped against the granite. But none of it seemed trashy or out of place, any more than the silent people who stood there, touching names and weeping.

Riding home on the Metro, he wondered about many things. Who the guide had been–someone's mother, perhaps. His own mother–had she ever been to the memorial? Without telling him, just to run her fingers across the warm stone? He could hardly believe that she had not gone, but if she had, wouldn't it have comforted her, the way it had comforted him? Wouldn't she have come home and told him and then taken him so that they could touch the name together? He so wanted now to tell her, to take her. He wanted to see her pale face mirrored in the shining granite. He wanted to see her thin fingers take strength from the crevices that formed his father's name.

They needed him. Dead or not. They couldn't keep living with the pretense that he had never been. They needed the life flowing from his memory—even if the memories were sad. Wasn't sad better than no feeling at all? Wasn't the anger of that day at Bethany Beach better than endless frozen years?

If she didn't need him, or didn't think she did, Park must tell her that she had no right to choose for them both. He needed his father.

"Where have you been?"

She had beaten him home. Park took off his jacket and hung it carefully in the closet instead of throwing it in the direction of the couch as he more often did.

"Park? Where have you been?" she called again from the kitchen. "I was worried. You didn't leave a note."

He went to the kitchen door. Randy's pale face was flushed from the heat of the stove. She cocked her head and gave a shy half smile.

"I went," he started, not wanting to pain her, but pushing the words out all the same. His own need was greater than the need not to cause her pain. "I went to see the memorial." Her eyes clouded. "The Vietnam memorial. I found his name."

She turned her back on him, as though busying herself with the supper. The Saturday casserole was already smelling up the apartment with onion and noodles and tomato sauce and hamburger. She began to tear lettuce. "How could you find it?" she asked at last. "There must be thousands of names."

"Fifty thousand," he said. "More than." She didn't turn around, but he went on, sure of her attention. "They have a book, like a map, an index. A woman showed me."

"Oh."

"You've never been?"

"Me? No."

"It's beautiful," he said. "And it made me know—" How could he explain? If he told her that after the vision, all the knights had gone in quest of the Grail, would she understand? No, he was sure she wouldn't. "It made me feel–it made me think–" She was silent. She was not going to help him, so he blurted it out like a three-year-old: "I gotta know him."

"He's dead."

"I gotta know about him."

She turned toward him then. "Oh, Park," she said. "Please–you don't know what you're asking."

"I read his books," Park said, jerking his head back toward the bookcase in the other room. "Most of them. And the poems." She stood unmoving, unblinking. "Other people have fathers every day. Can't I have a little piece of mine?"

"He died years ago."

"Then tell me about him," he begged her stiff body. "Please, Mom, I really need to know."

"I can't," she said, turning her back to him again, her body sagging a little, growing weaker as he watched. "Please understand, I can't, but–"

"Yeah?"

"He has–he had a family." She let out a sigh as loud as her words. "Maybe it's time."

He went to her then and put his arms around her and rested his chin on her shoulder. Her back stiffened again, resisting his embrace.

"Summer," she said, slipping lightly away from him. "Maybe you can go visit them in the summer. I'll have to write. I don't know what they'll say. They never," she gave a choked little laugh, "they never really approved of me. Poor little West Texas white trash coming into their family." She laughed again. "Generals and colonels and gentlemen Virginia farmers right back to the time of old George himself."

Park guessed she meant Washington, but he wasn't going to interrupt her to ask. Not now.

"It's been years since I've seen them, at least two years since I've heard anything." She stopped herself and jammed a salad bowl into his hands. "You'll have to be patient."

"Sure," he said, putting the salad on the dinette table. "I can wait. It's okay."

"It'll have to be," she said wearily. "Don't get your hopes up too much. A lot has happened since. They may not be thrilled, you know."

He didn't know. Of course they'd want to see him. He was the Fifth. He belonged in the family line.

Katherine Paterson

Katherine Paterson was born in China in 1932, the daughter of missionary parents, and spent her early childhood there. Educated in both China and the United States, she was graduated from King College in Bristol, Tennessee, and later received master's degrees from the Presbyterian School of Christian Education in Richmond, Virginia, and Union Theological Seminary in New York. Her works have been published in many languages, including Russian. She won Newbery Medals for Jacob Have I Loved *and* Bridge to Terabithia, *and the National Book Award for* The Great Gilly Hopkins, *among many honors in her distinguished career. She and her husband, the parents of four children, live in Norfolk, Virginia, USA.*

YOU HAVE TO TRUST YOUR HEART

Akram Ailisli

IF SARVAR HAD returned from the army at some other time of year, it's entirely possible he wouldn't have gotten bored quite so fast. But he came back to the village in autumn. Late autumn. The harvest had already been taken in, and his father's melon field was bare. The slopes, which were generally covered with grass the height of a man, had already been mowed right down to the last blade; the orchards had been picked clean, and the fallen leaves had been raked up and burned; a few ripe quinces hanging from the bare branches and some golden ricks of hay on the slopes at the collective-farm threshing floor were all that remained of the abundance of autumn in Buzbulak.

The first day he was back home, Sarvar walked around and managed to see absolutely everything he hadn't seen for three long years in a few short hours. He saw the girls and women carrying water from the spring as they always had, the men drinking tea at the local *chaikhana,* and the teenagers playing dominoes at the recreation center. He saw that, as before, his fellow villagers gathered under the plane tree in the evenings to discuss soccer and politics, then unhurriedly made their way home just as they had three years ago. They invited each other over to drink tea in exactly the same order, using the very same words as before the army. That evening, several people invited Sarvar over to drink tea, and he asked a couple of his buddies to come and visit him as well. On his way home, he saw the neighbor boys standing at the corner: they had already started smoking. And farther away, he noticed a new flock of whispering, giggling girls. He learned that they still called his father Agalar the Cat Foreman, and his mother, the Chicken Lady. And he was overcome by a desperate boredom. It was absolutely unbearable.

He realized he couldn't last out the winter in the village: everything would come to a standstill, and even the noise of an occasional car passing wouldn't break the monotony. Those high, snow-covered mountains that almost touched the sky would cut Buzbulak off from the rest of the world for three whole months. There would be nothing but home and the *chaikhana,* back home again, and the *chaikhana* once more. . .The thought of the long winter terrified Sarvar: he fell asleep in horror of the winter to come, and he dreamed of summer, of a warm, fresh summer night.

He was in the melon field, sleeping on a platform which was floating high in the air, and the field spread out below him. The field was flooded with pale moonlight, white as milk, and the big melons were sprawled all over the beds like a flock of white sheep resting. He gazed at the melons and suddenly noticed some shadows stirring at the edge of the field by the mountain. They looked like bushes but took on an eerie, ominous appearance: they were moving about and whispering to each other, plotting something. Suddenly, they all rose and dashed toward the field; from this pile of rounded figures that looked like bushes rose up an enormous shepherd in a felt cloak with a stick in his hand; he waved the stick in the air, and the white melons which had been dozing peacefully in their beds jumped up and went racing after the giant in the black cloak like a flock of white sheep. Sarvar wanted to scream, but he couldn't; he wanted to spring up, but he was frozen to the spot. At that moment, dawn came and the sky grew light. Sarvar could see that the shepherd in the black cloak was Ajdar. He was standing at the top of the mountain, waving his hand, and shouting: "Go to Baku! To Baku!"

So much for Ajdar and the dream, but when Sarvar got out of bed in the morning, it was perfectly clear to him that he wouldn't spend the winter in the village. He washed lightheartedly, ate quickly, and went outside. For a while, he stood by the house next to theirs, which had been deserted for ages. It was Ajdar's house: the courtyard was overgrown with thornbushes, and the roof was grown over with grass. Sarvar had found out Ajdar was in Baku at the *chaikhana*, and he had also learned Teimur was a vendor at the bazaar. Since Sarvar and Teimur had been in the same class at school, without saying a word to his father, Sarvar began making preparations for the trip. He didn't ask his mother for money, but began to buy what he needed on credit. He had never sold anything at the bazaar himself, but he had heard that almonds and walnuts were the most profitable foodstuffs to trade in. So without any ado, he set off to those of his neighbors who had almond and walnut trees.

He bargained and haggled and finally struck up a deal just like a real wholesaler: Auntie Shovkat gave him sixty kilos of walnuts, and Auntie Gyulgoz let him have fifty-five kilos of almonds. Sarvar managed to convince his mother to let him go and engaged her help in persuading his father. And all the while, Sarvar could see the enormous city of Baku in his mind's eye, although he had never been any nearer the capital of Azerbaijan than the suburb of Balajarakh which he had seen when he was being sent to the army. He could already imagine how he would make a fortune after he had learned the knack of bargaining at the bazaar: he would stroll about Leningrad in a new suit and coat with lots of money in his pocket and plenty of time to spare. He would go to all the places he had visited on the rare free days he had had while serving in the army there. For some reason he recalled a long ago event concerning Ajdar.

It was summer–the time when the melons were just ripening. The summer when a pullet disappeared from the metal chicken coop that was standing in the melon field. In the morning, as soon as the loss was discovered, Sarvar and his father searched the entire field, beating under all the bushes, but they didn't find so much as a feather. The next night, another pullet disappeared. So Agalar decided to stay awake all night and try to catch the thief. He hid in the bushes under the trees, rifle in hand, but he dozed off toward morning, and yet another chicken vanished into thin air. Agalar was fit to be tied, because obviously, the thief was a two-legged one: for no other living creature could take a chicken from such a sturdy metal coop. He could have cared less about the chickens now: it was a matter of honor. And it was just as obvious that the stealing wouldn't stop at chickens, for the melons were ripening.

Agalar thought about it for a long time, recalling all his sworn enemies in the village and even the shifty boys from the neighboring villages, but he couldn't figure out who the culprit might be. And Agalar never did catch the chicken thief: it was Sarvar who finally saw him. One night, he appeared in person in the melon field, and as if that weren't enough, he came right up to the platform. Agalar was already snoring away, but Sarvar was just lying there on his stomach looking down at the rows of milk-white melons glowing in the pale yellow light of the moon. Suddenly, someone called out his name. Sarvar jerked up; he was too frightened to speak and couldn't even call his father.

"Don't shout!" he heard someone whispering from below. "Come down here! Don't be afraid. It's me, Ajdar."

But the boy was so terrified he couldn't climb down. All he could do was raise his head and see Ajdar pressed to a post right below him. Ajdar was standing there with his finger pressed to his lips going: "Sh-h-h!" His tall thin frame was all concentration as he motioned the boy to silence. Ajdar reached out his hands, pulled the boy off the platform, and gently lowered him to the ground. They crossed the melon field in silence, and when they reached the very edge, Ajdar stopped.

"Sit down."

The boy did as he was told.

"Thank you for not raising the alarm," Ajdar said with a smile, patting Sarvar on the shoulder.

For a while, they sat looking at each other, not making a sound.

"You were really scared, weren't you?"

Sarvar didn't answer.

"Listen, can you bring me something to eat?" asked Ajdar suddenly. "I'm starving. And if you don't mind, be a good fellow and don't wake up the Cat Foreman. OK?"

So Sarvar rose quietly and went to get some food. He brought a hunk of goat's cheese and two big loaves of pita bread. After Ajdar had eaten, Sarvar asked him:

"Were you the one who stole the chickens?"

"Yes."

"They were looking for you all over the village!"

"I know."

"Five policemen came to try to find you."

"No kidding!"

"They asked us if we knew anything about you. My father said you were in Baku. Is that where you were?"

"Yes."

"Then why did you come back?"

"Some rat finked on me. The police got wind of my whereabouts, and I had to high-tail it out of there."

"What are you going to do now?"

"I'm going to hole up here for a while, then when the coast is clear in Baku, I'll go back there."

Sarvar didn't ask him anything else: the rest he knew quite well. Three months earlier, Ajdar, who worked as an inspector at the local cannery, had taken three thousand roubles from the company till, supposedly to buy plums for making preserves, but instead of buying the fruit, he had disappeared. Everyone in Buzbulak knew about it. And they all knew Ajdar had been seen at the bazaar in Baku as well. A lot of rumors about Ajdar had made the rounds in the village in the ensuing three months. And their neighbor Ajdar, whom Sarvar had seen every day for as long as he could remember, had been transformed in his imagination into some legendary brigand. Sarvar was terrified by his unexpected appearance, and he was afraid to sit with him alone in the melon field. The boy sat silently and thought long and hard before asking the next question:

"Where do you spend the night?"

Ajdar didn't answer the question at once, but stared long and hard into Sarvar's dark eyes until the boy was frightened by his gaze. Then Ajdar asked:

"Do you promise not to give me away?"

"Sure! I won't tell anybody!"

They walked for a long time until they reached a stand of bushes right at the foot of the mountains. It was known as the Snake Pit in the village. Here, in a thicket under the spreading medlar branches, surrounded on all sides by prickly blackberry bushes, Ajdar had made his lair. To reach it, they had to crawl under the bushes for ages. The undergrowth was so dense, the moonlight could not penetrate it, and only Ajdar's flashlight cut through the darkness, revealing bits and pieces of this mysterious realm. Finally, when the blackberries had thinned out a bit, Sarvar came to an opening, rose to his feet, and gaped in wonder: in front of the wattle hut Ajdar had made for himself was a glade from which the thorn bushes had been carefully cleaned away and the grass cut down. The earth was evened out, and even sprinkled with water. Beyond the hut, right at the foot of the mountain, a spring flowed from under a rock. Here, Ajdar had built a tiny dam, and the water sparkled under the moonlight like molten lead; by the fire was a sooty kettle and a few chicken bones.

All the things inside the hut were familiar: a quilted cotton jacket, a kerosene can and lamp, the bucket Ajdar's late mother had fetched water with, and a pot. All this had been brought from the village: Ajdar had sneaked into his house at night and taken what he needed.

Every single night for a month or six weeks, he would wait until his father had fallen asleep and creep off to the blackberry thicket. And every night, he and Ajdar would pick wheat, peas, or beans from the collective-farm field and make such a fine soup Sarvar had never eaten better since. Those were the happiest days of his life, although at times he was frightened–very frightened. It wasn't easy to keep the secret, because the police were still looking for Ajdar. Once, he even decided to reveal the secret of Ajdar's hiding place, but as soon as he got to the center of the thicket and saw the hut that so resembled a cobweb, all thoughts of giving Ajdar away vanished. By the light of the moon, Ajdar didn't look like an enemy or a spy at all: he was just tall, skinny Ajdar, and he looked like his mother, Auntie Khaver, if anyone.

He passed that whole month of September in terror and a kind of incomprehensible joy: sometimes they would sit all night by the fire and talk. That was fine for Ajdar, who had nothing to do but sleep all day. His eyes were even puffy from too much sleep. Sometimes he would weave strange objects that resembled baskets or buckets of sedge. He rebuilt the dam by the spring almost every day, and he even started making up poems from boredom!

Guard me, little orphaned hedgehog,
For I have made these woods my home,
Leaving land and friends and neighbors,
Through bushes like a fox to roam.

"Behold the rising moon, foul world . . ." was the first line to another of Ajdar's verses. He would sit in front of his hut staring at the moon and repeating that line over and over. He never finished the poem, so Sarvar didn't even find out how it ended.

Fall came, and the rains began. One dark night, Ajdar silently said farewell in front of the hut. He hugged Sarvar and soared swiftly to the very top of the mountain like a hawk. He stood there on the peak waving his hand and shouting, "Go to Baku!" over and over.

Now there they were standing face to face by the gate of the Baku bazaar. Ajdar had gotten very fat: his belly stuck out in front, and he had a double chin. His breathing was labored, and he wheezed as he looked angrily at Sarvar, who could not for the life of him understand what he had done to deserve the wrath of his old acquaintance.

"What the devil are you doing here?" were the first words Ajdar spoke.

"I brought some stuff to sell at the bazaar; I want to use the money I make to go to Leningrad."

Ajdar stared for a long time at Sarvar's neatly pressed trousers and at the pure white sweater with red spots peeking out from under his jacket. Such sweaters could only be knitted by the old women of their native village. He stared and stared, obviously thinking something over.

"Are you planning to sit at the bazaar and sell the stuff dressed like that?" Ajdar asked, taking a pinch of snuff from his pocket. He sniffed it and began to cough. When the long coughing spell was over, he asked hoarsely: "What did you bring with you?"

"Almonds and walnuts. A hundred fifteen kilograms in all."

"Where did you leave them?"

"With Teimur at the other bazaar."

Ajdar gazed pensively at the road for a while, then walked over to the edge of the sidewalk and stopped a taxi.

"Get in and bring all the nuts to me."

A short while later, the two of them lugged two enormous sacks out of the same taxi; they left the nuts at the bazaar with a man Sarvar didn't know and went out through the other gate. Wet snow was falling and melting as soon as it hit the ground. Steam was rising from the ground, and there was a damp mist. Ajdar hung his head in silence as he made his way through the dampness and rot, with Sarvar following in his wake. The newcomer wanted to ask where they were headed, but he didn't dare. He wanted to remind Ajdar of the chickens and the moon, of the hut at the foot of the mountains and even recite some of the verses he remembered; perhaps it would rouse a smile or even a chuckle from the older man. But Sarvar kept his mouth shut and was glad that he did. Ajdar might misunderstand him and think he was asking some favor in return for the assistance he had rendered so many years ago: I scratched your back, now you scratch mine. Thus, they walked in silence along the tram tracks until they had almost reached their destination. Finally, Sarvar could stand it no longer and blurted out:

"Look, Ajdar, I didn't come here to take you away from your business. I'll manage on my own. It's not my first trip to a big city, after all: I served in the army for three years in Leningrad, you know."

"Ok," replied Ajdar, and that was all he said.

They turned the corner and entered a courtyard. Before them stood an old one-story house with a glassed-in verandah. On the verandah was a grey haired woman ironing sheets.

Leaving Sarvar outside, Ajdar went into the house, had a word with the old woman and motioned for the visitor to come in.

"Well, you'll be staying here," he announced. Ajdar opened one of the two doors that led from the verandah. "This is your room, and there's your bed. Drink tea and have a good rest. If you want, take a walk or go to the movies. This is Margo. She's a Georgian and lives all alone. If you need any money, just ask her. Don't bother coming to the bazaar. I'll sell all your nuts myself."

This sort of welcome was not to Sarvar's liking: why couldn't he come to the bazaar? Ajdar was treating him like a child! In what way was he worse than Teimur? But he didn't dare disobey Ajdar for some reason; nor did he have the gumption to object.

So Sarvar wandered around the city all day long and returned only in the evening to wait for Ajdar. He was sure that his old friend would turn up. But he didn't come that night or the next morning either. Sarvar waited until noon and headed for the bazaar, but he didn't see hide nor hair of Ajdar there. Nor could he locate his sacks, though he searched the whole bazaar. The man they had given the nuts to had vanished. So Sarvar went back to Margo to wheedle Ajdar's address out of her, racking his brains to try to figure out what it all meant. But the old woman wouldn't tell him the address, although she certainly knew it. That left Sarvar only one recourse: to find Teimur. He went to the bazaar towards evening right before closing time, and there he found his old school chum.

"Listen, you haven't seen Ajdar anywhere, have you?"

"Yeah, sure I did. He left for Tbilisi this morning."

"What do you mean, he left?"

"Just that. He left, and that's that."

"Did he say anything about me?" asked Sarvar, ready to burst into tears.

"Yeah, he said that you should go back to the village as soon as you'd had your fill of Baku. He told me you'll never make a decent vendor. The bazaar's no place for you."

"And what about the money!" shouted Sarvar. "What did he do with my nuts?"

"I don't know anything about any money," Teimur replied coolly. "You'd have to settle that between yourselves. I'm only passing on what he asked me to. He said something else: that you were to leave on an odd day, because on odd days, a friend of his is the conductor on car number seven. He said you didn't need to buy a ticket. Just to tell the conductor he sent you, and you'd get a free ride home. The train leaves at one in the morning. Don't forget. The seventh car, and say Ajdar sent you."

If they hadn't been in the same class at school for ten years, the conversation would have ended then and there, but their talk continued. Somewhere towards the end of this exchange, Teimur slipped up and smiled ever so slightly. He tried to cover his tracks, but Sarvar realized at once that Teimur was telling a good deal less than he knew.

"Don't try to fool me," he told Teimur. "Ajdar no more left for Tbilisi than you or I did, and moreover, you know where he is as sure as I'm standing here!"

"That's a laugh!" replied Teimur, but he was obviously nervous. "No one ever knows where Ajdar is. He's been living here for ten years without a residence permit."

"Why are you running off at the mouth about Tbilisi? I can tell by your eyes that you're lying! Don't you have a shred of honor left?"

Teimur didn't reply, but Sarvar could tell he was hesitating.

"I always thought he was a human being." Sarvar said more gently. "If I had only known he was going to swindle me like this! Two whole sacks of nuts–over a hundred kilograms! He took them from me and vanished into thin air!"

"You should have sold them yourself! Why did you give them to him!" said Teimur.

"He didn't give me the chance to! Just took the nuts and sent me packing! I had no idea he was going to cheat me like this. What a son-of-a-bitch!"

Teimur didn't say a word. They silently cleared the goods off the counter, tied up the sacks, and turned them over to the watchman for safekeeping. That done, they left the bazaar.

"Do you see what kind of weather it is?" asked Teimur.

"Yeah, it's cold."

"Do you see how clear the sky is? Just like in Buzbulak."

"It's probably snowed there by now," said Sarvar. "When I left, it was raining."

"Ajdar always has attacks in this kind of weather," Teimur said unexpectedly.

"What kind of attacks?"

"You mean you don't know? Ajdar is a very sick man. He has a bad case of asthma. A terrible illness. As soon as it gets the least bit cold, he can't breathe at all. He never comes to the bazaar when it's like this. He usually sits it out in some restaurant waiting for the climate to improve. There's a little bar in a basement not far from the sea . . ."

"Do you think he might be there now?"

"He might be . . . Who knows? Only don't mention my name if you happen to find him there."

Sarvar didn't ask another question. He left Teimur and headed straight for the bar, and there, in a dark corner, he found Ajdar.

"Ah! So you went to Tbilisi, you wretch! Is that any way to treat an old friend?"

"Sit down and stop your fussing, Cat Foreman's son!"

"I didn't come here to sit with you! Let's go! I want you to give me back my sacks of nuts!"

Ajdar tugged at Sarvar's sleeve.

"Sit down! I don't have your nuts. I already sold them."

"Then give me the money, you worthless thief!" cried Sarvar, shaking his fist at Ajdar.

But Ajdar calmly pushed his hand aside.

"If you want to fight, wait till we go outside! But for now, sit down, Cat Foreman's son."

"Are you trying to insult my father?"

"If you want to know, I'd like to kick his ass for raising such a son!"

"It's too bad I didn't turn you in when I had the chance," Sarvar told Ajdar. "Then maybe you wouldn't have become such a sneak."

Ajdar wasn't offended in the least: he even burst out laughing. Then he asked:

"And what are you planning to do in Leningrad? Drop in on your girlfriend or sell something at the market there?"

"That's none of your business! Just give me my money!"

Ajdar was silent for a while, then he pulled a handful of almonds from one pocket and three walnuts from the other. He placed them on the table and looked sullenly at Sarvar.

"Do you recognize this?"

"Sure! I'll get my money out of you even if I have to cut your throat for it!"

"You can cut my throat later."

Ajdar picked up a walnut from the table. "Did you get these from Auntie Shovkat?" Sarvar looked up at him in amazement. "And I bet the almonds are from Auntie Gyulgoz. From the tree just beyond our fence where the last pussy willow is. There was a fig tree by it and a plum tree next to the barn by the wall. It used to bloom in the fall. Is the plum tree still standing?"

"Sure. What could have happened to it? It can't get up and walk away! Now stop playing with me, Ajdar, and give me the money.

"Is the pussy willow still there, too?"

"Of course, why wouldn't it be?"

"I first kissed Sona under that willow tree . . ."

Ajdar fell silent, then began wheezing like a bellows. His chest began to rattle, and through the terrible wheezing, he said to Sarvar:

"Tell that pussy willow Ajdar is dying!"

Suddenly Sarvar noticed that Ajdar's eyes were full of tears; he was crying. The tears rolled down his cheeks one after another and fell onto his jacket. Sarvar suddenly felt sorry for Ajdar and wanted to comfort him. He wanted to say something kind, but he couldn't find the words.

"What date is it?" asked Ajdar.

"The thirteenth."

"The thirteenth . . . It's been a lucky day for me."

"Let's go," said Sarvar. "They're closing already."

The two rose only after all the lights had been turned out. It had grown colder outside, and the puddles were covered with a thin crust of ice. The moonlit street was bright and totally empty.

"You should leave today."

"Why is that?"

Ajdar turned onto the boulevard and walked along the shore, not taking his eyes from the sea. He walked in silence for a long time, then he said:

"You'll never make a trader. You've got no business hanging around the bazaar."

"I have no intention of making my living at the bazaar!"

"Then why did you come?"

"I told you. I just wanted to make enough money for a trip to Leningrad to have a good time."

"I came here to have a good time, too. That was ten years ago, and I'm still having a good time."

"There's a difference, isn't there? I didn't steal three thousand roubles of company funds!"

The sound that issued forth from Ajdar's chest was terrible to hear. He bent over double with pain and leaned with all his weight on the metal railing. He coughed and wheezed, trying desperately to catch his breath. Sarvar stood next to him and cursed himself for what he had said. Ajdar straightened up with difficulty. He couldn't talk, so they stood there looking at the sea. The moon was suspended in the middle of the sky, and the sea glowed with a cool fire under its bright light.

"Did I offend you?" asked Sarvar, upset.

"No," replied Ajdar, "I'm not offended." With that, he began to cough again. "It's that money choking me," he squeezed out through the wheezing. "That damned three thousand is stuck right here in my throat, draining my life away. Don't think I didn't want to return the money. I had it in my hands hundreds of times. But I could never quite make up my mind to do it. First it was a matter of honor, and then it was already too late. I haven't had that kind of money for the past five years or so. I could make it in a minute if I wanted to, but I don't. I haven't the slightest desire to do so. My heart isn't in it, and you have to trust your heart, you know."

Then the conversation took on a calmer note.

"Why did you steal the money and run away in the first place?"

"I didn't run away with the money."

"How is that? Did someone steal it from you?"

"No one stole it."

"Then what was all the fuss about?"

"It was all Ali-oglu's doing. He works in the store, you know, and one day he came up short three thousand roubles. I was in love with his daughter, Sona, and I love her still. I dream about her almost every night. She came running to me in tears and said they'd taken her father to the police station. I couldn't help it. I gave her all the money that was in the cash box, then realized I was in for it. I wasn't afraid of getting arrested. I ran away because I was sure that if I stayed, the truth would come out in the end. Then, not long after, I found out that scoundrel was marrying her off to someone else. I thought I would die. If I had found myself in the village just then, I would have killed him. I even came once, but I couldn't bear to set foot in the village itself, because my heart was so heavy with grief, and you have to trust your heart."

Ajdar fell silent, and before Sarvar's eyes arose a vision of their native village and Ali-oglu's house and the shop where he worked, and his elder daughter Sona's plump, madcap children romping about.

"Let's go," he told Ajdar, because there was nothing more to say.

"Where?"

"Wherever you want."

"Then let's go to the train station."

They walked and walked over the crunchy snow that was gradually turning to solid ice from the cold, then Ajdar sank down onto a bench along the way.

"What time is it?"

"Twelve-thirty."

"That means there isn't much time left until the train leaves."

"Why are you trying to get rid of me so fast? Did you blow all my money, or what?"

"No, it's just that I see you could easily be stuck here and get caught up in all this mess."

"But Teimur hasn't gotten caught up in it."

"And he never will."

"So why do you think I won't be able to make it here?"

"Because you're not hard enough. You're not a son-of-a-bitch."

And with that, the conversation ended. They lapsed into silence once more. Suddenly Sarvar glanced at his watch and said:

"Let's go!"

"So you're really leaving? Honest?"

"When have I ever lied to you?"

Ajdar rose from the bench.

"The conductor has your money. Remember to go to car number seven. Teimur told you, I guess. There are five hundred roubles for you. He'll give you the money as soon as you arrive. Go straight down this street and don't turn anywhere. It leads right to the station. Go on ahead. I don't think I'll go with you. I'll stay here." After a short pause, he added: "All it takes is one slip-up, and then there's no turning back."

The money was all in tens–a whole pile of them wrapped up in a piece of paper torn from a notebook. On the paper was written in faint, tiny letters in pencil:

A trader you should never be,
Or else you'll turn out just like me.
When in my grave I'm laid to rest,
You'll see at last that I knew best.

Sarvar took the money from the conductor, stuffed it in his pocket, and read the note then and there. Then he folded up the piece of paper and put it carefully in his pocket, too.

Sarvar was not the least bit surprised that the note was written in the form of a poem, because when he was still in school, he had written a love letter to one of the girls in rhyme, and ever since then he had known that there were certain things which could only be said in verse.

Akram Ailisli

Akram Ailisli is a Soviet Azerbaijanian writer born in 1937 in the village of Ailis. He first appeared in print in 1955 and graduated from the Gorky Literary Institute in 1964. Ailisli is the author of several collections of short stories, including With Our Fathers and Without. *His cycle of novellas* People and Trees *describes everyday life in an Azerbaijanian village during the Second World War. He has translated the works of Chekhov and other well-known writers into his native Azerbaijanian and his own writings have been translated into many of the languages of the Soviet Union.*

THE PRETTIEST

Cynthia Rylant

ELLIE'S FATHER WAS a drinking man. Everybody knew it. Couldn't help knowing it because when Okey Farley was drunk he always jumped in his red and white Chevy truck and made the rocks fly up and down the mountains.

He had been a coal miner. Drank then, too, but just on weekends. A lot of miners drank on the weekend to scare away the coming week.

Okey had been hurt in a slate fall, so he couldn't work anymore. Just stayed home and drank.

Ellie was his youngest daughter, the youngest of five. She didn't look anything like Okey or her mother, both of whom had shiny black hair and dark eyes.

Ellie was fair. Her hair was nearly white and her skin pale like snow cream. Ellie was a pretty girl, but her teeth were getting rotten and she always hid them with her hand when she laughed.

Ellie loved her father, but she was afraid of him. Because when he drank he usually yelled, or cried or hit her mother. At those times Ellie stayed in her room and prayed.

One day Okey did a strange thing. He brought home a beagle. Her father couldn't hunt because his right arm wasn't strong enough to manage a rifle anymore. But there he was with a beagle he called Luke.

He made Luke a house. Spent the whole weekend making it and didn't even stop to take a drink.

Then Luke was tied up to his house, and he kept them all awake three nights in a row with his howling.

Okey would not explain why he'd bought a hunting dog when he couldn't hunt. He just sat on the porch with a bottle in his hand (he'd taken it up again) and looked at Luke.

Ellie was the only one of Okey's children who took an interest in his pet. The older girls were not impressed by a dog.

But Ellie, fair and quiet, liked the beagle and was interested in her father's liking for it. And when Okey was sober, she'd sit with him on the porch and they'd talk about Luke.

Neither of them could remember later who mentioned it first, but somehow the subject of hunting came up one day, and, hardly knowing she was saying it, Ellie announced she wanted to learn how to hunt.

Okey laughed long and hard. In fact, he had a little whiskey down his throat and nearly choked to death on it. Ellie slapped his back about fifty times.

The next time they sat together, though, she said it again. And this time more firmly, for she'd given it some thought. And Okey set down his bottle and listened.

He tested her. He set up some cans, showed her how to handle his rifle, then stepped back to watch. The first day she missed them all. The second day she hit one. The fifth day she hit four out of nine.

So when she brought up hunting again, they fixed the date.

They went out on a Saturday about five-thirty in the morning, just as the blackness was turning blue. Ellie was booted and flanneled like her father, and she had her own gun.

Okey held his rifle under his left arm. They both knew he'd never be able to shoot it. But neither said anything.

It was just getting light when they made the top of the mountains, their breaths coming fast and smoky cold. They each found a tree to lean against and the wait began.

Luke had traveled far away from them. He was after rabbit, they knew that much, and they were after squirrel. Okey told Ellie she might have half a chance of hitting a squirrel. Rabbit was out of the question.

Ellie flexed her fingers and tried not to shiver. She was partly cold and partly scared, but mostly happy. For she was on a mountain with her father and it was dawn.

Neither Okey nor Ellie expected a deer to come along. So neither was prepared when one did. But less than twenty feet away, stamping its front hoof in warning, suddenly stood a doe. Okey and Ellie looked across the trees at each other and froze themselves into the scenery.

The doe did not catch their scent. And she could not see them unless they moved. But she sensed something was odd, for she stamped again. Then moved closer.

Ellie looked at the animal. She knew that if she shot a deer, doe or buck, her father would never stop bragging about it. "First time out and she got a deer." She knew it would be so.

The doe was nearing her tree and she knew if she were quick about it, she could get that deer. She knew it would be easier than shooting a squirrel off a tree limb. She could kill that deer.

But she did not. The doe moved nearer; it was a big one, and its large brown eyes watched for movement. They found it. Ellie raised her arm. And she waved.

The deer snorted hard and turned. It was so quickly gone that Ellie could not be sure in which direction it headed.

"Godamighty!" she heard Okey yell. She knew he might be mad enough to shoot her, if he could hold on to his rifle. She heard his crashing across the ground.

"Now wasn't that," Okey gasped as he reached her tree, "wasn't that the *prettiest* thing you ever seen?"

Ellie hesitated, wondering, and then she grinned wide.

"The *prettiest,*" she answered.

And they turned together and went quickly down the mountain to find Luke and go on home.

Cynthia Rylant

Cynthia Rylant was born in 1954. Her novel A Fine White Dust *is a Newbery Honor Book. She is well known for her texts for picturebooks, two of which,* The Relatives Came *and* When I Was Young in the Mountains, *are Caldecott Honor Books, and her poetry (*Waiting to Walta: A Childhood*) and her collections of short stories,* Every Living Thing *and* Children of Christmas: Stories for the Season. *She is also the author of* A Blue-Eyed Daisy. *She lives in Kent, Ohio, USA.*

FROM THE EDITORS

A Word about Soviet Children's Literature

Soviet children are well acquainted with the classics of American literature. The one-hundred-volume series of World Literature, including many American classics, has been popular for several years, as has the fifty-volume series of Adventure Novels, including Mark Twain and James Fenimore Cooper.

All publishing in the Soviet Union is coordinated by the State Committee of Publishing. In 1987, 620 million books were in circulation for children. By 1995 it will be up to 950 million, with over thirty percent of all publications in the country for children. Yet there are never enough books published to satisfy demand, even though most first printings of popular authors are a half million to a million copies. Most new books, all sold at cost, are completely sold within two or three weeks.

The publishing committee publishes books in sixty-eight foreign languages, in addition to the national languages of the various Republics of the USSR, making a total of 120 languages. All books are sent to the over 360,000 public and school libraries in the Soviet Union.

Children's-book writers in the Soviet Union are often prominent public figures who work actively on behalf of children. Their works are used regularly in the schools to educate and give moral guidance. Many writers hope that children will learn the values of peace and cooperation from their stories.

Soviet children's books contain an invitation for the reader to write to the author or publisher, and most books elicit over 30,000 letters per year, all of which are answered. Children frequently ask questions about friendship, love, and how to establish better relations with their parents and teachers. Authors and publishers then use this information to determine what to write and publish in the future.

INDEX OF AUTHORS

ACKNOWLEDGMENTS

Grateful acknowledgment is made to the following for permission to reprint from previously published material:

"Brother Leon" by Robert Cormier: Excerpted from *The Chocolate War* by Robert Cormier. Copyright © 1974 by Robert Cormier. Published by Pantheon Books. Reprinted by permission of the author, Pantheon Books, Victor Gollancz Ltd. and Curtis Brown Ltd.

"Homesick" by Jean Fritz: Excerpted from *Homesick: My Own Story* by Jean Fritz. Copyright © 1982 by Jean Fritz. Published by G. P. Putnam's Sons. Reprinted by permission of the author, G. P. Putnam's Sons, and the Gina Maccoby Literary Agency.

"Carrying the Runaways" by Virginia Hamilton: Originally published as part of *The People Could Fly: American Black Folktales* by Virginia Hamilton. Copyright © 1985 by Virginia Hamilton. Published by Alfred A. Knopf, Inc. Reprinted by permission of the author and Alfred A. Knopf, Inc. All other rights retained by the author and Alfred A. Knopf, Inc.

"The Treasure of Lemon Brown" by Walter Dean Myers: Copyright © 1983 by Walter Dean Myers. Originally published in *Boy's Life,* March 1983. Reprinted by permission of the author.

"The Story of the Blue Beach" by Scott O'Dell: Excerpted from *Carlota* by Scott O'Dell. Copyright © 1977 by Scott O'Dell. Published by Houghton Mifflin Company. Reprinted by permission of the author and McIntosh & Otis, Inc.

"The Black Stone" by Katherine Paterson: Excerpted from *Park's Quest* by Katherine Paterson. Copyright © 1988 by Katherine Paterson. Reprinted by permission of the author and Lodestar Books, an affiliate of Dutton Children's Books, a division of Penguin Books USA Inc.

ACKNOWLEDGMENTS

"The Prettiest" by Cynthia Rylant: Excerpted from *A Blue-Eyed Daisy* by Cynthia Rylant. Copyright © 1985 by Cynthia Rylant. Published by Bradbury Press. Reprinted by permission of the author.

"Bullet" by Cynthia Voigt: Excerpted from *The Runner* by Cynthia Voigt. Copyright © 1982 by Cynthia Voigt. Published by Atheneum Publishers. Reprinted by permission of the author.

"The Boy Who Drew Unicorns" by Jane Yolen: Copyright © 1988 by Jane Yolen. From the book *The Unicorn Treasury* compiled and edited by Bruce Coville. Published by Doubleday, a division of Bantam Doubleday Dell Publishing Group, Inc. Reprinted by permission of the author, Bantam Doubleday Dell Publishing Group, Inc. and Curtis Brown Ltd.

Grateful acknowledgment is also made to Vsesojuznoje Agentstvo po Avtorskim Pravam (VAAP) for permission to translate and reprint "Wild Rosemary" by Yuri Yakovlev, "You Have to Trust Your Heart" by Akram Ailisli, "Quiet Morning" by Yuri Kazakov, "Traffic on Sadovoi Road" by Victor Dragunsky, "The Tubeteika Affair" by Vytaute Zilinskaite, "The Joke" by Radii Pogodin, "Fortune's Favorite" by Gunars Cirulis, "None of My Business" by Anatoly Aleksin, and "Edžiņš" by Vilis Lacis.

Acknowledgments

Jacket manufacturing donated by
New England Book Components, Inc. Hingham, Massachusetts

Paper provided by Perkins & Squier Company, Book Publishing Papers

Jacket paper donated by Lindenmeyr Book Publishing

About the Editors

Anatoly Aleksin was born in 1924 in Moscow and graduated in 1950 from the Moscow Oriental Institute. Besides being a popular writer, he is also a prominent public figure. Mr. Aleksin is President of the Association "Peace to the Children of the World," vice president of the Soviet Peace Committee, and a frequent representative of his country to international meetings promoting the welfare of children. His literary biography appears on page 163 of this book.

Thomas Pettepiece, born in 1944 in Texas and raised in California, is a graduate of UCLA, Garrett Theological Seminary, and has done graduate work in International Development. He is the author of *What Everybody Already Knows* and *Visions of a World Hungry* and writes children's stories. Mr. Pettepiece is an Emmy Award-winning television commentator, has produced films and curriculum, and consults on global education. Presently, he is president of the Soviet American Co-Publishing Project and president of PeacExpo, an organization which promotes global understanding and cooperation. He formerly served on the National Board of Directors for the U.S. Committee for UNICEF.